The Undercover Cowboy

The Undercover Cowboy

A Twilight, Texas Novella

LORI WILDE

AVONIMPULSE
An Imprint of HarperCollinsPublishers

This is a work of fiction. Names, characters, places, and incidents are products of the author's imagination or are used fictitiously and are not to be construed as real. Any resemblance to actual events, locales, organizations, or persons, living or dead, is entirely coincidental.

Excerpt from *The Christmas Dare* copyright © 2019 by Laurie Vanzura.

THE UNDERCOVER COWBOY. Copyright © 2019 by Laurie Vanzura. All rights reserved. Printed in the United States of America. No part of this book may be used or reproduced in any manner whatsoever without written permission except in the case of brief quotations embodied in critical articles and reviews. For information, address HarperCollins Publishers, 195 Broadway, New York, NY 10007.

Digital Edition SEPTEMBER 2019 ISBN: 978-0-06-231153-5
Print Edition ISBN: 978-0-06-231154-2

Cover design by Nadine Badalaty
Cover photograph © Jacobs Stock Photography Ltd/Getty Images

Avon Impulse and the Avon Impulse logo are registered trademarks of HarperCollins Publishers in the United States of America.
Avon and HarperCollins are registered trademarks of HarperCollins Publishers in the United States of America and other countries.

FIRST EDITION

19 20 21 22 23   HDC   10 9 8 7 6 5 4 3 2

To Rachael, the loveliest of angels.

Chapter One

IN RETROSPECT, ALLIE GRAINGER probably shouldn't have been texting and walking across Main Street during the eleven a.m. cattle drive.

Her bad.

In her defense, her bestie, Tasha, had just been dumped by the love of her life, and Allie was nothing if not a good friend. Unfortunately, Tasha texted while Allie was on her way to a job interview during her lunch break from her receptionist's position at the Twilight, Texas, Visitors Center.

Allie was strolling past a living diorama of Twilight's colorful past—shirtless Wild West reenactors portraying rugged cowboys by shoeing horses, repairing wagons, and pitching hay. A throng of camera-clicking gawkers surrounded them.

Normally, she would have slowed down for the eye

candy. She appreciated a hunky cowboy as much as the next girl, but today, her mind was half on Tasha, and the other half on her impending interview at the popup art gallery inside the old courthouse.

The job was temporary, but if she landed it, she'd finally be using her art degree and it would be a feather in her résumé cap. Plus, the added income would keep her from having to move back in with her parents. At least until she could find another roommate.

The day was miserably hot. Soaring over one hundred degrees already with no relief in sight. Perspiration collected on her brow and in her cleavage. So much for shower fresh.

Over the last few days, the electric coop that supplied the town and rural areas had been suffering rolling blackouts from the strain of overworked air-conditioning systems. Two nights in a row, she'd awoken in complete darkness, sweaty to the core. Mom used the blackouts as an excuse to try to lure her back to Dallas, but Allie could handle a little heat.

Her thumbs flew over her smartphone Head down, she stepped off the curb, as she texted: How R U holding up?

Tasha's text bubble exploded with poop emojis.

Allie's heart twisted for her friend, who just last week, believed her boyfriend, Tag, was on the verge of proposing. Shitty. Got it. Anything I can do?

An gif of an angry woman chasing a wide-eyed, wild-haired, screaming man with a rolling pin popped onto her screen.

Allie wrote: He's not worth the jail time.

A second text box flashed onto the screen, this one from her mother. Good luck with the interview. Fingers X'd.

Thnx, Allie texted.

???, Tasha texted back.

Allie: Oops. That was 4 my mom.

Tasha sent a yellow, smiley-faced, eye-rolling emoji.

Mom: Allie? U there?

Allie: Mom, stop the helicopter.

Mom: Just wanted U to know I'm in your corner.
And if U don't get the job, U can move back
home. Dad and I will pay for your PhD.

Allie blew out her breath. No way in hell-o. She punched in: TY. I'll call U after the interview.

Tasha: Huh?

Fiddlesticks, she'd texted the wrong person again. Gotta go, Allie wrote to both Tasha and Mom, her thumb posed over the arrow that would send her reply.

But she never got a chance to push it.

A loud booming noise shattered the lazy summer morning. Sharp and sudden.

Crack!

She jerked her head in the direction of the noise. Was someone shooting off Fourth of July fireworks ten days early? Or was it a gunshot?

Rumbling shook the earth. People gasped as the sound of galloping hooves thundered across the ground. The dozen head of cattle, trotted out daily for tourists in Twilight's recent bid to compete with the Fort Worth Stockyards, had been on their way down Main Street toward their grazing pasture in a ranch off Highway 51. The boom had jolted them, and they'd outpaced their drovers.

And they were stampeding straight toward *her*.

Allie's mouth dropped open, and the steamy morning air, mingled with dust kicked up from the cattle, rushed across her tongue.

Run!

But she couldn't move. The faint dings of fresh text messages sounded from the cell phone still curled in her palm. Heat rose off the asphalt, mixing with the pungent aroma of cowhide. The bulging, frightened eyes of the charging longhorns stared right through her.

Uh-oh.

Run! Run!

Rubbernecking sightseers were lined three feet deep on the sidewalks framing the newly widened thoroughfare. The sea of bystanders leaned forward on a collective inhale like spectators at a rodeo, curious to see if the champion bull rider had eight seconds in him. Or if the bucking bull would bash his head.

"Run! Run! Run!" the crowd screamed.

Too late.

The cattle were already there. No time to get out of the way.

If Allie hadn't been lucky by fate, and optimistic by nature, she might have lost her cool. But her childhood stint in the cancer ward had taught her an important lesson, and she did what she'd always done when things got tough.

Calmly, she closed her eyes, said a prayer of gratitude, and waited for a miracle.

THE WOMAN STOOD in the middle of the road with such stunning calm. Her face turned to the sky, eyes closed, seemingly oblivious to the stampeding cattle bearing down on her. She was either a full-fledged crackpot, dumb as a fence post, or suicidal.

But when it came down to it, what did it matter? She was in the path of disaster.

Undercover detective Kade Richmond wasn't supposed to call attention to himself, but if someone didn't do something fast to save the loony lass, she was going to get flattened by the small herd of terrified longhorns.

Kade didn't hesitate. He threw down the hammer he'd been using to pound out a horseshoe against an anvil, shoved through the gawking horde, and sprinted to the middle of the street.

Without a second to spare, bellowing cattle bearing down on them, Kade scooped her into the crook of his arm—*thank God she was petite*—hoisted her against his hip, and ran as fast as her weight—and his cowboy boots—would allow.

Which wasn't quite fast enough.

Just as he reached the curb, a longhorn caught him, clipped his shoulder, spun him full circle, and sent a jolt of searing pain down his arm.

Jelly beans and jawbreakers, that hurt.

Kade stumbled, staggered against a huge old pecan tree root growing up out of the sidewalk. The sweet-smelling bundle in his arms made a soft sound of distress. His gut clenched like an angry fist and his pulse pounded in the back of his throat.

Had he hurt her?

His intentions had been honorable and succinct. Distressed damsel. Rescue her.

But now?

Her breasts were pressed flat against his side and the hard beads of her nipples were making him feel things he had no business feeling.

Unnerved, he set her down beside the tree and put a hand to her shoulder to steady them both.

"Oh," she whispered. "*My.*"

He stepped back and studied her. His mind was addled, rattled. All he could think about was how good she looked in that skimpy white skirt and filmy navy blouse with a heart-shaped cutout at the center of her cleavage.

Was she even wearing a bra?

C'mon, Richmond. He had no business letting his thoughts graze freely. He was nothing to her, just the chump who'd risked blowing his cover to save her pretty little fanny. Time to let her go and get back to work.

Cameras flashed. Cell phones clicked. The chattering crowd surrounded them.

"What a hero!"

"This is so going up on Facebook."

"*Mamas,* do *let your babies grow up to be cowboys.*"

Well, dammit, so much for anonymity.

He kept a restraining hand on her elbow and looked down into eyes so blue they were almost purple. Her lips were the color of fresh strawberries, plump and red and shiny. Her skin beneath his hand was warm, delicate, yielding.

"You okay?" he asked, his tone coming out unexpectedly brusque as he straightened. The shade from the pecan tree overhead provided scant respite against the late-June heat.

She blinked, and those purple-blue eyes framed by black lashes so thick they could double as paintbrushes knocked his heart sideways. Her gaze caught his, brushfire hot.

Kade's head spun, fast and dizzy. That bugged him. He hated feeling out of control. Dehydrated. That was it. He'd been standing in the relentless sun all morning, pretending he was a blacksmith in 1885. He was dehydrated. Had to be it. This little slip of a thing couldn't shove him *that* off-kilter.

"Thank you," she murmured.

"You should watch where you're going," he said, still sounding like Billy Goat Gruff. "You almost got creamed."

She bobbed her head as if she agreed, but she was already sneaking a peek at her cell phone screen.

Kade grunted. Some people never learned.

She made a sudden clucking sound with her tongue, and he thought of the way mother hens called to their young. "You're hurt!"

"What?"

She reached out cotton-candy-pink fingernails to touch his shoulder. "You're bleeding."

The sharp tip of the longhorn had jabbed his skin where his right arm attached to his shoulder. One long, shallow slash. No biggie. No stitches needed. He'd had much worse in his rodeo days.

Kade tugged a red bandana from the back pocket of his jeans and awkwardly tried to tie it around the cut with his left hand.

"Here," she said in that throaty voice of hers. "Let me."

Before he could tell her "no," she'd already plucked the bandana from his hand and was dressing his wound.

The crowd *oohed* and *aahed* and took more pictures, and that was when he realized they thought her rescue from the stampeding herd was part of the living diorama.

He resisted an eye roll. *Tourists.*

The drovers had gotten the longhorns under control

and were guiding them toward the ranch. End of excitement. The tourists started dispersing.

The woman bent her head as she tied a knot in the bandana, and he could smell her scent, an oddly compelling combination of watermelon, lemons, and honeysuckle. Her fingers were quick and competent.

His stomach pitched and dipped.

"There you go," she chirped and patted his biceps.

"Thanks." His voice came out rough as a cheese grater.

"Thank *you*," she said. "For being in the right place at the right time."

"What's your name?" he asked. Why did he want to know? The sooner he got back to his undercover assignment the better.

"Allie." Her smile was as bright as a halo. "Allie Grainger."

"Ka—" He stopped himself before he gave his real name and supplied his undercover alias. "Rick Braedon."

"Nice to meet you, Rick. Thank you for saving me." She sent him a coy glance as if she might be interested, and by damn, he was certainly interested. But then without another word, she turned and disappeared into the crowd.

Leaving Kade to wonder if he'd imagined the whole damn thing. His arm tingling strangely where she'd touched him.

"May I take a picture with you?" asked an elderly

woman who was holding up a camera. "I traveled all the way from Pittsburgh to have my picture taken with a real live cowboy."

Because he couldn't think of a way to get out of it gracefully, Kade agreed. Besides, from this angle, he had a pretty good view of the side entrance of the courthouse. The place he had under surveillance. The place the FBI suspected was about to be hit by an art thief during the upcoming Fourth of July art festival.

The very same place that sweet, clueless Allie Grainger had just stepped inside.

Chapter Two

WITH THE SOUND of Rick Braedon's rich, deep voice tickling her ears, Allie grinned her way into the courthouse that no longer served court. The historic building was alive with the sound of saws and hammers, sheetrock dust, and booted men in hard hats and tool belts.

See there. If she just had faith that everything would work out for the best, it always did. Not only had she *not* been trampled by cattle, she'd met a cute guy too. And speaking of things working out for the best, she decided she was going to ace this job interview.

That was until she followed the directional arrow signs posted along the scaffolding route through the construction zone and walked into the makeshift office built from cubicle dividers.

A dozen people, most of them around her same age, crammed into the small space and tried not to look desperate as they filled out applications, fidgeted, and checked their electronic devices.

There was no place to sit, barely any room to stand. The aged air-conditioning system wasn't up to the task and the improvised room was uncomfortably warm. Several people had sweat stains ringing their armpits.

Allie slipped around the hipsters, millennials, and a couple of senior citizens applying for the low-wage job, excused her way up to a cheap folding table pretending to be Ikea, and slanted her cheeriest smile at the bored, Cheeto-thin young woman bouncing on a yoga ball in lieu of a chair.

"Hi," she said, hoping she sounded like the right kind of cheerful. "I'm Allie Grainger."

The ennui-infused woman, whose mouth was slick with vampire-red lipstick, didn't bother glancing up from the kittens-swatting-yarn YouTube video playing on her tablet. "Fill out an application and take a seat," she intoned.

Allie turned on her cell phone to check the time. Yipes! Fifteen minutes until she had to be back at the Visitors Center. The encounter with the cowboy had taken a big chunk out of her thirty-minute lunch break.

"Mmm." Allie leaned in. "I know you're like . . . um . . . super busy, but I was wondering how long the wait is? I've got to get back to work."

Ennui woman gave Allie's starched white skirt a fishy stare and then flicked her gaze to her four-inch stilettoes—that Allie had worn intentionally so she'd looked taller. According to statistics, tall people were more likely to get the job.

Allie lengthened her spine, held Ennui's gaze.

A calculated look crossed the woman's face as if she was trying to decide something important about Allie. "Do you know Lila?"

Um. No. No, she did not. "Who's Lila?"

Ennui tapped her chin with a fingernail that was the same shade of red as her lipstick, studied Allie for a long moment, opened her mouth, closed it, and then finally said, "You look like you should know Lila."

Was this some kind of code? Was she being led to lie about knowing Lila? Allie frowned, not sure how to proceed.

"I bet you *do* know Lila," Ennui said.

Huh? What was going on? *Did* she know someone named Lila? Allie searched her memory. Nope. Nothing. "I'm pretty sure I don't know a Lila."

"Maybe you know her by her middle name? Emily. You *do* know Emily, don't you?" Ennui winked as if they were in on a conspiracy.

The wink made her feel included, part of a secret club. Allie liked the feeling, but this was one of the weirdest conversations she'd ever had. She cocked her head. "I *do* know a couple of Emilys."

"There you go." The woman pushed up from her yoga ball. It bounced against the cubicle wall with a soft *thwap*. "Follow me."

Allie glanced around at the other people waiting for

an interview. Several of them glared at her. This wasn't fair, cutting in line, and pretending to know Lila Emily. "I can't . . . I shouldn't . . ."

"Do you want a shot at this job?" Ennui hiss-whispered.

"Yes, but I don't want to cheat anyone else out of a chance."

Ennui straightened, her uber-red lips shining in the light dripping in through the window behind the cubicle wall. "Never mind. This was a mistake. Fill out the application and get in line."

Allie thought of having to call her mom to tell her she needed to move back in. Imagined how happy her mom would be, hovering, cooking her meals, washing her clothes, snooping through her cell phone. Compared that loser feeling to the triumphant coup she'd feel when she took her parents out to dinner at Del Frisco's to tell them she'd finally landed a job in her chosen field.

She didn't understand what was going on with this weird interview, but she desperately needed the job, for her mental health if nothing else. "Please don't write me off. I want a shot."

"Well, then, come along." Ennui tossed her head and guided Allie past the other applicants who were shooting eye daggers at her.

Why was she getting special treatment? Had her folks pulled strings? But how could they? She hadn't told them the details of her job interview, precisely because she didn't want them pulling strings.

Gulping, Allie ignored the urge to slump guiltily past the other interviewees. She tossed her head like she belonged, and kept her eyes straight ahead, aloof as a runway model. Jumping ahead of the line went against every egalitarian bone in her body, but when life handed you an advantage, it was dumb not to take it.

Right?

It wasn't as if she hadn't had her share of disadvantages. Still, guilt had an uneven weight, a thorny texture, and the pasty taste of cold oatmeal.

"This way." Ennui turned to crook a finger, stopping briefly in front of a columned entryway leading into the dark recesses that once upon a time had been a courtroom. She switched on her cell phone, using it as a flashlight, and crossed over the threshold.

Allie hesitated at the sill where the bare concrete they'd been walking on merged into mahogany hardwood.

Shadows stretched before her, thick and mysterious. The intoxicating fragrance of oil paints on canvas dizzied her head. She curled her fingernails into her palms, giddy with the pelt of scents—the woody aroma of pencils, the ashy odor of charcoal dust, the earthy essence of clay. It smelled like art school. Like coming home.

Her heartbeat quickened.

"C'mon," Ennui prodded, sounding faraway and ghostly, the beam from her cell phone bobbing several yards ahead of Allie.

This was the direction life was guiding her. She'd

learned a long time ago not to fight the current, to surrender to the flow. Taking a deep breath, she exhaled slowly, and hurried to catch up with Ennui.

Lumps of things loomed on either side of the pathway cordoned off by thick velvet ropes—pallets stacked high with boxes, sheets covering exhibits, the spindly bones of metal scaffolding. An eerie, unsettled sensation crawled and wriggled down her spine. Weirdly, she was having a hard time inhaling. The darkness was too heavy, almost solid.

Breathe. Trust.

At the far end of the room shimmered a faint filter of light, coming through what appeared to be a door cracked ajar. It seemed like something from a recurrent nightmare where she was running from toothy monsters she couldn't see and got mired in honey-slicked floors.

She knew construction workers were in the midst of setting up the makeshift museum, but you would think someone would turn on some lights, or take down the heavy curtains and let the sunshine in.

"Hurry," Ennui's voice snapped sharply. "I don't have all day."

Spurred, Allie picked up the pace, her heels clicking loudly against the hardwood floor. She reached Ennui just as the woman turned toward the thin beam of light.

Indeed, a door to what was once judge's chambers was propped ajar, wedged open with a thick hardcover edition of a classic art textbook.

Ennui paused and took hold of Allie's arm. "Piece of advice—if he thinks Lila sent you, you're much more likely to get the job."

Um, so keep up the lie? Allie shifted her weight, felt guilt roll up the back of her throat. What if she lied and the "he" in question called this Lila person?

Before Allie could respond, Ennui knocked on the open door. "Dr. Thorn," Ennui called. "I have found a suitable candidate."

The door swung all the way open, and Allie blinked against the stun of sunshine. A middle-aged, professorial man pushed a pair of leopard-print reading glasses up on a ski-slope nose. His forehead was oversized, his ears undersized. His hands were tiny, fingers stubby, but his feet were long and wide. Both tall and stout, he duck-walked toward them with an uneven gait, his knees bowed from the weight of his girth. He was oddly assembled, like he'd inherited the wrong combination of ancestral DNA.

"This is Allie Grainger," Ennui said and shot Dr. Thorn a meaningful glance. "*Lila* sent her."

And then Ennui disappeared like some fairy-tale sprite. One second she was there, the next she was gone. It was creepy, and frankly, a little unnerving. Especially now that Allie was alone with the strange-looking man who eyed her up and down with a speculative stare.

"Hal Thorn," he said and stuck out an extraordinarily dry palm. On his pinky finger he wore a big gold ring.

Allie didn't really want to shake his hand, but she did. His palm was almost as small as hers.

"Have a seat." He waved at a folding chair surrounded by books and boxes and stacks of empty art frames. Beyond a wealth of bookcases there was no other furniture in the room.

She stepped over a pile of unopened packages and perched on the edge of the metal chair with her knees together, her purse clutched in her lap.

"So," he said, and squatted in front of her, eye level. She was surprised that he could crouch and wondered if he was going to be able to stand up afterward. It was stuffy in the room, and far too warm, but he wore a nubby brown cardigan and he wasn't perspiring. "Lila sent you."

His ice-water-blue eyes pierced into her, his gaze a clinical laser. Exact. Sharp. Dangerous.

Allie cleared her throat, and extended her resume, which was pitifully short, toward him. "Actually, I—"

"I don't need to see a résumé," he said. "If Lila vetted you, you're in."

Stomach churning a cocktail of thrill and chill, Allie cocked her head. "I'm hired?"

"Can you start tomorrow?"

Wow. Okay. Yes. "I work at the Visitors Center from ten to four-thirty," she said. "But the job listing did say you were looking for evening help."

"That's right. From five until we close at ten p.m. through the month of July. If things work out, I'll consider offering you a permanent job traveling from city to city helping me put on these popup art galleries. Would you be interested in that?"

"Yes!" She jumped to her feet, forgetting for a moment she had essentially lied to get the job. "Yes, I accept."

Hal Thorn laughed, showing a row of crooked, egg-shell teeth. He straightened, rising up from the squat with the agility of a yogi. "While I love your enthusiasm, Ms. Grainger, I'd be remiss if I didn't bring up salary before you accepted."

"Oh, right." She pressed three fingers over her mouth to keep from giggling. She wasn't expecting much. It was an entry-level job in a competitive field.

"Twenty dollars an hour."

That much? Was this for real? The job listing had quoted half that salary.

"The wages might be more than you were expecting," he said, his frost-colored eyes drifting back to her face.

She nodded.

"That's because you'll have special duties."

Uh-oh. Allie bit her bottom lip. Was that code for something unsavory? "What do you mean?"

His lips thinned into a shifty smile. "Besides being a guide at the museum, I'll need you for courier duties. Driving things back and forth from the main museum to the popup. Do you have a car?"

"Yes." She let out a soft sigh. Whew, for a minute there she thought he was going to suggest an indecent proposal.

"Would you also be available on your days off from the Visitors Center, and before your ten a.m. shift?"

"Yes, absolutely."

"No other demands on your time?"

"Other than the Visitors Center, I'm all yours."

"No boyfriend?"

Ick, was it getting creepy again? "No boyfriend."

"Good. No distractions. I can see why Lila recommended you."

Allie cringed. Did she come clean now and kill the job offer? Or keep her mouth shut?

"Welcome aboard, Ms. Grainger." Dr. Thorn shook her hand again. "We're happy to have you. I'll walk you out."

Instead of taking her out the way Ennui had brought her in, Dr. Thorn ushered her to a side entrance. He leaned in close, his freaky blue eyes pinning her to the spot as he stared into her like a human lie detector. "Tell Lila I said hello."

Allie gulped, hitched her purse up on her shoulder, nodded. "Will do."

Dr. Thorn reached out to squeeze her wrist, gave her a curly smile. "Report to Daphne at eight a.m. tomorrow morning. She'll get you set with Human Resources and show you the ropes."

"Daphne?"

"The young woman who escorted you in."

Oh, yes, Ennui. "Will do."

He waved to her and went back inside. Allie turned

to head back to the Visitors Center with two minutes left of her lunch break to spare. She blinked against the sunlight after the dimness of the building.

And there, leaning against the pecan tree and drinking a bottle of iced tea, was the shirtless, sweaty cowboy who'd saved her from being trampled.

His sultry gaze met hers, dark eyes shimmering black in the heat of the noonday sun, and he stared at her as if he knew her most shameful secret and every lie she had ever told.

Chapter Three

KADE WATCHED THORN touch Allie's wrist, and his blood cooled twenty degrees. Since he'd seen her go into the courthouse, he'd convinced himself it was a coincidence, and she had nothing to do with Thorn.

He liked her. His gut liked her. And Kade could usually trust his gut. Neither he nor his gut wanted her to be mixed up with Professor Thorn.

But there she was, looking suspiciously chummy with the man suspected of orchestrating the thefts of valuable works of art across eleven states. Just because she was looking chummy with Thorn didn't make her one of his confederates.

Maybe not. But hanging out with Thorn put her squarely in the FBI's crosshairs.

Over the course of the past three years, eleven minor

masterpieces had been stolen from the popup museums at festivals, holiday celebrations, and street fairs across the country, the originals replaced with flawless forgeries.

So flawless that the thefts had gone undetected until number eleven this year during Mardi Gras in New Orleans.

Putting Thorn on the FBI's radar.

Art expert, and frustrated artist himself, Professor Harold Thorn was the architect of the trendy popup museum concept. The idea was to pair up-and-coming local artists with regional masterpieces and hold the events in diverse and unlikely settings with the stated aim of bringing art to a wider audience.

Thorn had a flair for dramatic staging and the events had been an unqualified success. Overall museum attendance had shot up following the popup events. But with the discovery of the forged George Rodrigue in New Orleans, Thorn had fallen under suspicion. It wasn't until the FBI started digging into his background that the thefts of the other ten paintings were discovered.

The FBI was certain that Thorn was involved, or if not him, one of the people in his employ, but they had no proof and his credentials were impeccable. Thorn came from old money and seemed to have no motive to steal the paintings with a total worth of less than three hundred thousand dollars.

Thorn had several art degrees, was a sought-after

lecturer, and had never been in trouble with the law. He had tenure at a private university in upstate New York, and several of his students had gone on to become renowned artists. Why would he steal lesser works of art?

As of yet, none of the stolen paintings had been found on the black market, at least not that the FBI had been able to track.

The museums that had been hit were mortified that they hadn't discovered the forgeries at the time the thefts occurred, and they were reluctant to go public. Only the stolen Rodrigue had been in the news.

Which led to Thorn's next stop at the Cowboy Palooza Fourth of July Festival in Twilight, Texas.

The most valuable painting scheduled to appear in Thorn's gallery was a Remington worth somewhere in the neighborhood of half a million dollars, the most valuable piece to appear in a popup. The Sid Richardson Museum in Fort Worth was willing to let the FBI use the Remington as bait to catch the culprit or culprits as long as they had enough agents on the ground to ultimately prevent the theft.

Lack of media attention made for the perfect setup for an undercover sting on Thorn's event during the long Fourth of July weekend. The FBI had enlisted help from the Hood County Sheriff and the Twilight Police Department for around-the-clock surveillance of Thorn, his employees, and the popup art gallery.

Based on Kade's undercover experience in vice with

the TDP, and his stint as a bull rider in the PBR, he'd been selected for the undercover assignment of posing as a cowboy in the living diorama in the town square.

His goal?

Be the one to nail the art thief.

Why did he care so much?

He was up for promotion and vying against four other candidates. Doing well on this assignment with the Feds would give him a leg up on the competition. And he was itchy for the position. He was tired of vice, tired of being in the field, tired of making his living in the world of lies and deception.

Once upon a time, he'd enjoyed living behind the mask of a made-up identity, thrilled to play cat-and-mouse games with criminals, but four months ago, his world was turned upside down.

He'd been undercover as a bouncer, investigating gang activity operating out of a strip club called Tits-a-Poppin' on the Hood–Tarrant County border, but he'd been unable to penetrate the group's inner circles until he befriended one of the strippers, who was the main gang leader's girlfriend.

Angi was a sweet kid who'd started stripping her way out of poverty and got caught up with the wrong crowd. He'd felt badly about deceiving her. It ate at him like an ulcer, ugly and raw. She vouched for him with the gang, and because of her, he was able to infiltrate them and get the evidence he needed to put the gang leader behind bars. After the gangster was arrested, Kade promised Angi protection if she testified against her boyfriend. She was terrified but agreed to do it.

Tragically, before he could get her to a safe house, she jumped from a fifth-story window to her death. Kade knew it wasn't suicide, but he hadn't been able to prove it. The gang leader was still awaiting trial, but Kade was worried that without Angi's testimony, the gangster would go free.

Guilt had been his constant companion ever since Angi's death, and he couldn't help feeling responsible. Undercover felt more and more like a straitjacket, and he was desperate to Houdini his way out of vice.

Thorn was his ticket out.

One last lie, nail Thorn, and he could be free.

Kade pushed away from the pecan tree, holding the iced tea bottle between his finger and thumb, and strolled toward Allie.

They'd made a connection. He had an edge. This was his chance to get close. See what he could find out about her association with Thorn.

She stopped short, her eyes widening, face going pale, teeth sinking into her bottom lip like she wanted to bolt.

Why? Was she feeling guilty about something?

"Hey there," he said.

"Um . . ." She raised a hand with a faint smile. "Hey."

"You okay?"

"Yes, why wouldn't I be?"

"You had a scare with the longhorns."

"Are *you* okay?" She nodded at his shoulder, still wrapped with the red bandana she'd tied there. "You're the one who got poked."

He shrugged. "I've had worse."

"Thanks again." She smiled that dazzling smile that got tangled up inside his head. "For saving me."

"My pleasure," he said, and meant it. This was the best day he'd had in a long time, and her smile was the reason why.

She started walking again, and he fell in beside her.

"What are you doing?" she asked, her tone shifting from friendly to cautious.

"Making sure you get safely across the street."

"I appreciate the concern." She hitched her purse up on her shoulder, notched her chin in the air. "But you don't have to worry about me."

"It's no trouble."

"The street's clear." She spoke in a quick clip that matched her steps. "The cows don't come back until four."

"The cattle."

"What?"

"The cattle. Cows are strictly female, and that herd is mostly steers."

"Oh," she said. "Good to know." She was outpacing him, already to the curb, but his legs were twice as long as hers and it only took two serious strides to catch up.

"Listen," he said, unnerved by how breathless he sounded.

"I gotta go." She stared straight ahead, watching the

road, which was good, but he wanted to see her eyes so that he could get a read on her. "My lunch break is over. I'm late getting back to work."

"Where do you work?"

"The Visitors Center," she said, then added with a sidelong glance in his direction, "and now at the popup gallery."

His stomach dipped, flipped. So, Thorn had hired her. What did that mean? He narrowed his eyes, trying to figure out if she was part of Thorn's crew or a hapless victim.

"You'll be crossing the road every day going from one job to the next?" He cocked his head.

"I will."

"Could you do me a favor?"

She slanted him a sidelong glance, pursed her lips. "What's that?"

"Promise me you won't text and walk anymore."

She threw back her head and laughed. He liked how she was able to poke fun at her foibles. "I promise."

"'Cause I'll be here for the next two weeks. Watching you walk back and forth across the street." He heard his voice lower, fill with testosterone. Felt his heart punch hard against his chest. "Until after the Fourth of July."

"I'll be on my best behavior," she promised. "I don't want to cause you any more trouble."

No trouble at all, sweetheart. That rash thought burst like an overfilled water balloon inside his head. *Jelly beans and jawbreakers, what's going on here?*

They were across the road now and halfway up the sidewalk toward the Visitors Center.

He stopped. "Allie?"

She kept walking, but hesitated at the steps leading into the building, turned around, and fixed those big blue eyes on him.

His heart did a full somersault.

"Yes, Rick?"

Rick?

Kade blinked and it took him a full ten seconds to remember his undercover alias. "Would you like to grab some dinner tonight?" He hadn't meant to ask her out. It just happened.

A soft smile touched her lips and her eyes turned dreamy. "That's so sweet of you to ask, but a friend of mine is going through a tough breakup, and tonight she needs a shoulder to cry on."

"Tomorrow night?" he asked. *Knock it off. You shouldn't be courting a potential suspect.*

"I start my job at the popup tomorrow evening."

He stood there trying to look cool and nonchalant. "When will you be free?"

She shook her head, looked rueful. "Honestly? Not until after Cowboy Palooza is over."

Yeah. That was too late. He was thinking maybe he could pick her brain about Thorn. Find out what she knew . . . or what she could find out *for* him.

"Ah, well," he said and tipped his Stetson to her. "Guess we're just two ships passing in the night."

"Or two cattle drives passing on the trail." She grinned, waved gaily, and pushed her way into the Visitors Center as if they hadn't just had a cosmic encounter.

Leaving Kade wishing like hell that Thorn hadn't hired her.

Chapter Four

ALLIE SPENT THE rest of the afternoon answering visitors' questions in between calling and telling her mom about the job and texting Tasha about meeting up for drinks at the Horny Toad Tavern for happy hour.

Her mind was a tumble of emotions—empathy for Tasha, joy over her new job, guilt for the whole Lila business, elation that Rick had asked her out, and disappointment that he hadn't pushed harder for a date.

By the time five o'clock rolled around, she was ready to celebrate her new job with a strawberry margarita and Horny Toad nachos. But tonight was all about Tasha. Allie had made up her mind to suppress her own good news. Plenty of time for that after she helped Tasha get over Tag.

Allie slipped out of her stilettoes and into comfy walking shoes to hike the mile from the Visitors Center to the

Horny Toad Tavern. The afternoon was a scorcher, and by the time she pushed through the swinging wooden doors of the establishment, she felt like a wilted petunia.

Mopping sweat from her brow with the back of her head, she nodded to the regulars playing no-stakes poker at the front table and took the stairs to the newly added second-floor bar and grill.

It was cooler up here and the vibe more millennial than the slower-paced downstairs where GenXers and Baby Boomers tended to congregate. The room was packed for happy hour, or what Tasha had now dubbed "sad hour." On the stage, positioned against a wall with lots of windows, a guitarist was tuning up. The smell of cumin and chili powder set Allie's mouth watering.

Mmm, nachos. She'd skipped lunch because of the job interview and she was starving.

Allie inched her way up to the bar, ordered a strawberry margarita and the nachos, put her credit card on the bar, and glanced around for Tasha. She pulled her phone from her purse and saw that Tasha had texted.

Too blue, Skipping sad hour. 4give me.

Allie texted back. Definitely not. U can't let Tag win. Get your butt over here.

Tasha texted a gif of Eeyore shaking his head.

Rats. When Tasha got like this, dynamite couldn't blast her out of her reclusive mood. Allie was about to text that she was on her way over when the bartender slid her margarita across the bar.

"Run a tab?" he asked.

Not now. She shook her head and he picked up her credit card to run it.

She texted: Please come out.

Tasha: I'm a mess. Crying all day.

Allie: He's not worth your tears.

Tasha: He's my soul mate.

Allie: You can't tell by the way he's treating U.

Tasha didn't answer.

Allie took a long sip of margarita. Oh, gosh, the perfect blend—sweet, tangy, and cold. She sucked down a big gulp. Got a brain freeze. Clutched her head. Ow. Ow. The brain freeze ebbed and when she focused again, she texted: Tash? U there?

Tasha: Oh Allie, I just answered the door to a beautiful bouquet of flowers.

Allie: From Tag?

Tasha: He's so sorry.

Allie: Don't fall for pretty flowers.

Tasha: Gotta go. Tag is calling.

Well, fiddlesticks and fried rice. She wanted her friend to be happy, but she doubted Tag's sincerity. Should she leave and go over there? Or keep her nose out of Tasha's business?

The bartender returned her credit card and she tucked it into her pocket as she debated what to do about Tasha.

"Could I get the nachos to go?" she asked the bartender.

"Hey, *ba*-by," slurred a drunken male voice. "Don't rush off."

Allie rolled her eyes. She didn't have to glance over to know it was Stanley Lipscomb, a Horny Toad regular who had hit on every female who came into his sphere of orbit. He was from a wealthy ranching family, a former SMU quarterback, and thought he was God's gift to the universe.

"You here all alone?" Stanley slung an arm over her shoulder and leaned in close, almost knocking her over with his whiskey breath.

"Hands off, Frat Boy," she growled, and tried to pull away.

"Aw, c'mon, don't be that way, Princess." He tightened his grip on her shoulder.

Allie's pulse sped up. Stanley was a major jerk, but for the most part, she'd considered him a harmless drunk. "Listen, Stanley," she said, trying a perkier track. "You know I'm not your type. You like 'em tall, dark, and stacked."

"True," Stanley mused with a luminous leer. "But I'm thinking maybe I should give short, blonde, and cute a tumble."

"Nah, I'm not really feeling it."

"Oh?" Stanley chortled. "You wanna feel it?" He yanked her flush against his body, grinding his hips against her, making sure she felt his erection.

"Please," she said, her throat tightening, her voice coming out high and strangled. "Let go of me."

"Not until you give me a kiss." He thrust out his tongue, waggled it.

Allie froze. What now? Throw her drink in his face? Stomp on his foot? She couldn't knee him in the 'nads like she wanted because he was holding her too tightly against him.

Breathe. Trust.

She closed her eyes, inhaled. Sent up a prayer. The bouncer had to be around here somewhere.

"You heard the lady," growled a flinty, masculine voice. "Let go of her."

Allie's eyes popped open. There stood Rick Braedon, hands on his hips like he was a sheriff toeing off with Bad Bart. Or in this case, Bad Stanley. Her heart pivoted, leaped.

"And if I don't?" Stanley challenged, jutted out his chin.

"Oh, you're making this too easy." Rick knotted up his fist, and with a quick, solid punch, smacked Stanley squarely on the nose.

"Yowl!" Stanley howled. Blood spurted from his nose like a faucet, both hands leaving Allie's waist as he raised them to staunch the flow. He swore a blue streak, using every curse word in the book. "You broke my nose!"

Heads turned. Eyes stared. The room went silent.

"Are you all right?" Rick turned to Allie.

She nodded. From behind Rick, she saw Stanley fist his hands and snarl, blood streaming down his cheeks.

Before she could cry out a warning, Rick sidestepped smoothly, just as Stanley lunged. The drunk landed face first onto the wooden floor.

"Sumofabitch!" Stanley's curse was muffled as he spat out a mouthful of blood.

People were laughing and catcalling, amused to see Stanley get his comeuppance.

"I'm suing," Stanley blubbered. "You can count on that."

"You do," said the bartender, "and we'll all testify against you. It's about time someone punched your ticket, fool."

The people circled around the bar nodded in unison.

"Wanna get out of here?" Rick murmured, offering Allie his elbow.

She nodded and stepped over Stanley's prostrate body on their way to the door.

"Mop!" the bartender hollered to one of the waitresses. To Stanley he said, "Stop bleeding on my floor, Lipscomb."

Stanley let loose with a fresh string of curses, but the sound was cut off by the door closing behind them. Rick escorted her from the Horny Toad, and out onto the street clogged with tourists.

"Thank you." Allie pulled from his grip. She stood there, the late-afternoon heat searing down on her head as hot as a flat iron.

Rick tipped his Stetson. "You're welcome."

"Do you make a habit of going around saving damsels in distress?" she asked. "It seems to be your schtick."

"Nope," he said. "You're special." His dark eyes looked deeply into hers. She felt the impact like a jackrabbit's kick, unexpectedly hard and solid.

Oh, hell, what was *that*?

Something alarming occurred to her. "Did you follow me here?"

He shook his head. "I'm not a stalker."

So he said. His magnetic eyes were unreadable. Her pulse sped up, ticking faster and faster, a mysterious train of excitement and danger rushing through her.

"Thanks again," she said and stepped away from him, holding out her hand a bit stiffly. Distance. She needed distance from this handsome man.

An amused smile barely curled the corners of his angular mouth. "I'm walking you to your car."

"That's not necessary."

"There's a bleeding frat boy upstairs that says differently." He slanted his head, studied her through half-lowered eyelids.

He had a point. Stanley might hold a grudge and it would be easier for him to take it out on her without Rick beside her.

"I didn't drive. I live nearby."

"Then I'm walking you home," he said in a gravelly, no-argument tone that sent her heart fluttering in a totally enjoyable way. "Let's go."

He took her arm again and she melted at his touch. Partly, because the weather was so hot, and partly because he was being all take-charge and alpha male-y.

"Where do you live?"

Should she tell him? He was a stranger. But he had rescued her . . . *twice* . . . and he had a trustworthy face.

"The Goodnight," she said, referring to her apartment complex a few blocks away.

He glanced over at her, head cocked at that appealing angle again. "No kidding? I just moved in."

What were the odds? Now, that was happy coincidence. She was a big believer in serendipity.

"We're neighbors?" she asked, startled by how gleeful she sounded. "I'm in the west wing."

"East for me."

"How long have you lived there?" she asked.

"A week. You?"

"Since I finished my master's degree in May. It's my first place."

"Graduate school, huh? How old are you? I thought

you couldn't be more than nineteen, but then I saw you in the Horny Toad ordering a margarita, so I figured you had to be at least twenty-one."

"I'll be twenty-four on August 30." She eyed him up and down. "How old are you?"

"Twenty-nine."

"When's your birthday?"

"April 7."

Aries, the ram. A fire sign. She was Virgo, earth sign. Did they match? Not that she really believed in horoscopes or anything, but she was curious.

"What did you get you master's in?" he asked.

"Don't judge," she said as a preemptive strike. She was tired of people making fun of her degree. "I have an MFA in visual arts and a BA in art history."

"Why would I judge you?" He seemed truly perplexed and that made her like him all the more.

"Because it's such a competitive field, and my chances of getting a job that pays a living wage are slim to none."

"But you love it?"

Her skin warmed at the kind expression on his face. "More than anything!"

"I'd say anyone who judges you is just jealous because you're doing something you love."

"Um, not really." She scratched her chin that was getting itchy from the sun exposure. She should have reapplied sunscreen before walking over from the Visitors Center. Or maybe the itchiness was from the intensity of his stare.

"You just got a job at the popup art gallery. That's a big deal."

"Yeah, well, it's temporary." She thought about the Lila thing, and winced. "And something of a fluke."

"A fluke? How's that?"

"Here we are," she said, stopping on the sidewalk leading into the Goodnight. "You to the east and me to the west."

The building, like most everything in the Twilight town center, had been constructed in the late 1800s. The Goodnight was an old hotel recently converted into apartments; keeping the old-world charm of old-fashioned lift elevators and exposed brick walls and combining them with modern amenities for the hippest complex in Twilight.

"I'll walk you to your door," Rick said in that same commanding tone.

A fresh thrill skipped through her. Oh dear, she liked him too much.

He opened the front door for her, and she was grateful for the cool blast of air that greeted them.

They walked through the common area that had once been the lobby of the Goodnight Hotel. The furnishings were cowboy chic—wood and leather, hide and bronze, rustic wagon wheels and antler chandeliers.

"Thank you again for defending my honor with Stanley," Allie said when they reached the dual iron-cage elevators across from each other. One went to the west wing, the other to the east.

"Door-to-door service," he said, leaning around her to push the button for the elevator to take them to the west wing. Her wing. He smelled of sunshine and sandalwood and starch.

She couldn't stop herself from inhaling a deep whiff and savoring his scent.

The elevator settled with a clang and he ushered her inside. It was small, and cramped, built for the meager demands of the nineteenth century. A bit claustrophobic to be honest. It could hold up to a maximum of eight people if the occupants crowded shoulder to shoulder.

"Which floor?" he asked, his long index finger hovering at the panel.

"Four. Top floor."

"I live on the fourth floor too. On the other side of the courtyard, of course."

"Small world."

Silence fell over them as the elevator groaned and jerked upward on the rising pulleys.

Allie stared down at her shoes, feeling a bit self-conscious now that she was completely alone with the stranger who'd rescued her twice in one day. A handsome stranger. A good-smelling stranger. A stranger she wanted to know better.

Maybe she should see if he wanted to try again for a date. She turned toward him. "Listen—"

But she got no further. The elevator jerked, jolting so hard it slammed Allie's teeth together.

She lost her balance and stumbled forward just as the elevator shuddered to a stop and the lights went out.

Rick's arms slipped around her waist. "I've got you," he whispered, his voice a daring life preserver in the steamy darkness.

Chapter Five

THE SEXY FILLY was driving him crazy.

Kade had caught Allie as she fell. Her sweet face landed in the crook of his elbow, her soft breasts smashing against him. His mouth went drier than the Sahara Desert as he tried not to notice.

He was on assignment. He was getting close to her to find out more about Thorn, but here, in the heat and the dark of the closed space, work was the last thing on his mind.

Right now, all he could think about was her short, flirty, do-me-big-boy skirt and those dynamite legs, and how explosive they would feel wrapped around his waist. If they were dating, he'd run his hand up the hem of that skirt, feel those creamy thighs and . . .

Whoa! They were *not* dating. In fact, they barely knew each other. He would *not* be touching creamy thighs, but damn, she was killing him, smelling so nice and succulent. He wanted to—

Don't be a caveman.

Yeah, easy to say. Much harder to do when a woman who revved his engines like a Ferrari was in his arms.

Start with that. Get her out of your arms.

Kade released her, slowly loosening his grip, not letting go all the way until he was sure she was steady on her feet.

She let out a little sigh . . . of disappointment? Or was that his projection?

The woman was a suspect. He could not forget that. He knew better than to get personally involved. He worked vice, for crying out loud. Women had offered him sexual favors to look the other way, but he'd never once been tempted to compromise his integrity.

Until now.

Until Allie.

What was going on? Why, more than anything in the world, did he want to yank her back into his arms and kiss her until neither one of them could breathe?

What was it about her that turned him on like no woman ever had?

What indeed?

There was a naivety about her, a wide-eyed, Bambi-on-a-ten-lane-freeway-in-rush-hour-traffic quality to her. Seriously, how could someone as warm and open and trusting as her be involved with an art-theft ring?

Oh, shit. He'd lost his objectivity. Criminals came in

all shapes and sizes and personality types. He'd arrested Sunday-school teachers dealing weed at potluck socials, and Girl Scouts shoplifting makeup from Walmart. Looks were deceiving, and when it came right down to it, no one could be trusted.

"Rick," Allie whispered, her voice lifting up at the edges, crisp as the whites of a fried egg.

Huh? Rick? Who was that?

Oh, yeah, his alias.

"What is it?" Kade murmured, his head dazed, dreamy. He had to snap out of this or he was going to make a big mistake.

"Why did the electricity go out?"

"I'm guessing it's another rolling blackout. With the heat wave we've been having—"

"How long before the electricity comes back on?" Her voice stretched out, long and taut.

He made a beats-me face before he remembered she couldn't see him in the dark. "I'm sure it won't be long."

"Shouldn't the generator kick on soon?"

"I don't think there's enough power in the generator to run the lifts."

"Oh." Her breath bubbled out in a long swoosh.

"Something wrong?" he asked.

"Um . . . I'm a tiny bit claustrophobic."

"How tiny?"

"Not very. In fact, I'm a lot claustrophobic. I was just trying not to make things worse."

The last thing he needed was for her to have a full-blown panic attack. He shifted into law enforcement mode. Her safety was his first and only concern. "Are you under the care of a doctor for anxiety?"

"No," she croaked. "Not anymore."

"But you were?"

"Once. A long time ago."

"How long?"

"Nine years. I've been good. Great even . . ." Her voice grew wispier, thin as smoke.

"Are you on any medications?" he asked.

"Not currently." She paused, her breath chugged.

"Breathe deeply and hold it," he said.

She inhaled sharply, but he could hear that she was only breathing from her upper chest and not her diaphragm.

"Breathe from your belly," he coached.

"I can't," she said. "It feels like I'm trying to suck air through a straw."

Jelly beans and jawbreakers, he was compounding the problem. "All right," he soothed. "Just hold your breath."

Suddenly, the elevator was utterly quiet and Kade realized he was holding his own breath too. Somehow, the silence heightened all his senses. "Now blow out your breath like you're trying to blow out birthday candles. Get all the air out of your lungs."

He exhaled forcefully to demonstrate, and she followed suit, finished with a gasp and a cough.

"Good job."

"You sound like a doctor," she said, adding, "or a cop."

The hairs at the back of his neck lifted. Did she know? *Simmer down, Richmond. You're tipping your hand.*

She was leaning against him, arms wrapped over her chest, squeezing herself in tight. Her knees were trembling so hard her entire body shook.

"Here." Gently, he put a hand to her shoulder. "Let's sit down."

"Okayokayokayokay."

She was wound up like Foamy the Squirrel. He guided her to the floor, sinking down with her to the bottom of the elevator. He could feel tension coursing through her muscles.

"You're not alone. I've got you." He slid his arm around her and she dropped her head to his shoulder. "That's right. Let go, sweetheart."

Sweetheart? Cowboy, you're sliding in deep.

But she was quivering and crumpled, and she strummed every heroic bone in his spine. This was not good.

"You're safe, you're safe, you're safe," he chanted, felt his heart beating in time to his words.

Danger. He was treading on dangerous ground.

But his body didn't give a damn.

From the darkness, the song "Don't Worry, Be Happy" burst into the elevator. Kade jumped. "What the hell?"

He heard Allie fumble with her purse. "It's my mother."

"'Don't Worry, Be Happy' is your ringtone for your mother?" he mumbled.

"It's my ringtone for everything."

"Seriously?" Was Miss Rose-Colored Glasses really that cheery? The more he learned about her, the less likely it seemed that she was involved with the art thefts. Still, she had accepted a job with Thorn . . . reason enough to keep his eye on her.

"Shh," she hissed, her cell phone flashing luminously in the blackness, and then in a chirpy tone said, "Hey, Mom."

"Where are you?" her mother asked, speaking so loudly that Kade could hear her. "Are the lights out where you are? Are you okay?"

"I'm fine," Allie said. "Why are you yelling?"

Her mother lowered her voice and Kade had to tilt his head closer to Allie and her phone to pick up what her mother was saying. "The lights went out. This is the first time the blackout has hit here in Fort Worth. I called to make sure you're okay. Are you in the dark?"

"No," Allie lied glibly.

Hmm, Kade mused. So, she wasn't above lying.

"Mom," Allie said. "I gotta go."

"Congratulations again on your new job. I can't wait to hear all about it."

"Bye, Mom." Allie punched the end button. Sat with the cell phone in her lap. The light illuminated her face. A frustrated, rueful smile crossed her lips. "Sorry," she said. "My mother is a tiny bit overprotective."

"How tiny?" he asked.

"Not very." She laughed and met his gaze above the

puny light from her cell phone screen. "Did you just start a running joke with me?"

He lifted one shoulder, couldn't resist matching the heat of her warm smile. "Looks like your panic attack has passed."

"Mom'll do that to me," she said.

"What? Snap you out of a panic attack?"

"Yes." Allie rolled her eyes. "I can't afford to show her the slightest sign of weakness or . . ."

"Or?"

Allie shook her head, her soft curls bouncing around her shoulders. "She'll smother me."

"Only child?" he guessed.

"Yes, but it's more than that."

"Oh?" he said, trying not to look like he was milking her for information.

"It's a long story."

"We may be here awhile," he said. "No telling how long the blackout will last. We could be here all night."

Her breathing quickened and her body stiffened beside him.

Bright move, Richmond. You're scaring her back into a panic attack. "But it will most likely only last a few minutes," he amended.

"How few?" she asked.

He chuckled, delighted that she could rouse her sense of humor under the circumstances. "I wish I could give you a firm answer."

She sighed and sank her back against the elevator wall.

"Are you okay?" he asked.

"Not you too," she groaned.

"Me too?"

"I can take care of myself, *Mom*."

He wasn't so sure about that. Not from what he'd seen so far. He shuddered to think what might have happened if he hadn't intervened with the longhorns and the creep in the bar.

"I know you haven't seen me at my most kickass," she said, reading his mind. "But I'm resilient. Unfortunately, because I'm small, people see me as a dainty, helpless thing and they often feel the need to rush in and save me without giving me a chance to save myself."

"Is that comment directed at me?"

She crinkled her nose, looking like an adorable, blonde Easter bunny. "Well, you are trapped in an elevator with me because of your Sir Galahad syndrome."

"My what?"

"Seriously, you know it's true. Don't even try to deny it. I mean, c'mon." She held up two fingers. "Twice in one day? Either you have a thing for perceived damsels in distress, or you really like me."

Kade grunted. She had a point. On both counts. "Are you saying you didn't need me to push you out of the way of that stampede?"

"That's right."

"If I hadn't shoved you aside, you would be in the hospital right now, and that's best-case scenario."

"Oh, my." She laughed, low and winsome. "You do think a lot of yourself, don't you? Any number of things could have happened. None of which have anything to do with you."

"Like what?" he challenged.

"The cattle could have swerved and missed me."

"Clearly, you don't understand the nature of the herd mindset."

"Clearly," she said, pulling her spine up a bit stiffly, "you don't understand *me*."

"Gotta plead guilty on that charge." He jammed fingers through his hair, tossed his head. "The cattle would not have swerved."

"Did you know the Mythbusters did a piece where they put bulls in a china shop, and not a single piece of glass got broken? Apparently, animals with hooves can pivot a full 360 degrees, which means they can turn sharply in one quick motion, graceful as a pirouetting ballet dancer."

"That doesn't mean they could have avoided you in a stampede when there was nowhere for them to pivot to."

"Okay, fine. Let's assume you're right. They're about to flatten me and you aren't around."

The image of her little body, smashed and bleeding, lying in the middle of Main Street popped into his head. Kade grunted.

"I might have jumped aside," she said.

"You had your eyes closed!"

"I was listening," she said compassionately, as if he were a backward child who couldn't grasp the multiplication tables.

"For what?" he sputtered, flabbergasted.

Her enigmatic smile was filled with delight and otherworldly wisdom. "Why, the Voice that tells me what to do."

That look on her face, the quality of her tone, the shift in her body language, all knocked the pins out from under him. She *believed* that nonsense. He felt both incredulous and strangely jealous of her capacity to believe.

And trust in that belief.

"Don't look at me as if I'm crazy," she said. "Just because you've never experienced contact with a higher source doesn't mean it doesn't exist."

"Uh-huh," he said, unable to keep sarcasm from burning a hole in his throat. "You're entitled to believe whatever you want. Just like I'm entitled not to believe it."

She giggled, actually *giggled* at him.

"What's so funny?"

"Oh, Rick, you just don't get it. I don't believe . . . I *know*."

He raised a hand, an eyebrow, and his doubts as he waved dismissively. "Whatever."

"Are you so closed-minded about everything?"

"When it comes to woo-woo stuff . . . let's just say I'm a realist."

She made a noise that sounded a lot like pity.

Seriously? She was feeling sorry for him? Kade bristled. Her cell phone screen dimmed, winked out, plunging them back into total darkness.

"I should have charged it before I left work," she muttered.

"I've got my phone. But let's leave it off for now. We might need it later and I don't know how much battery life I have left."

They sat in silence. In darkness. Touching shoulders. Breathing at the same pace and tempo. It felt good. Intimate. Special.

Honestly, too special and too intimate.

"That long story about why my mother is so overprotective," she said. "Would you like to hear it?"

"Why not? We're not going anywhere."

She leaned her head on his shoulder again, the pressure light and rewarding. She smelled of sunshine and rainbows and he supposed if unicorns were real they would smell like her—honest, genuine, sweet . . . special.

Kade realized with a start that she was about to tell him one of her most life-altering experiences. No hesitation. Simply open up and talk. So easy . . . just like that. Again, he was struck by competing emotions. Envy that she was so in touch with her feelings and didn't fear expressing them, and frustration at how naively she confided in a stranger.

"Not everyone you meet is your friend," he cautioned.

"I know that." She snuggled closer. "But *you* are."

"How the fu—" He broke off before he dropped the f-bomb. He respected her too much to use it around her and that rattled him. "You just met me. How can you know I don't mean you any harm?"

Her voice was shiny and warm in the hot elevator, soft as melted butter and full of things that scared him. Things like hope, belief, and love.

"That inner voice that you were making fun of told me that you could be trusted."

"Allie," he said. "You don't have to tell me your darkest secret."

"It's not really a secret. I just don't talk about it much because the past is the past and it doesn't really matter now except to explain why my mother is so helicoptery."

He started to tell her that she didn't owe him any explanation, but damn it all, he had a job to do. While he was ninety-nine percent sure she wasn't in cahoots with Thorn, she *was* working for him. If Kade handled things right, he could use Allie as his eyes and ears inside the inner workings of the art gallery.

But what if he was wrong? What about that one percent chance that Allie was an art thief who was turning the tables on him? What if his cover had been blown and Thorn had hired her to distract him? Maybe that was why she'd stopped dead in the street in the middle of the stampede in the first place. Maybe the whole thing had been a setup to lure him out.

Was he really that cynical? What about the guy at

the bar? Had that just been a show for his benefit as well? *Christ.* He'd been working vice for too long. He suspected everyone of everything.

"When I was twelve," Allie began, "I was diagnosed with a rare blood cancer."

The word "cancer" sliced through him like a knife, cold and sharp and deadly. "Al," he said, "that sucks."

"Hey." She laughed, a happy sound in the small elevator. "You just gave me a nickname."

"No one else calls you Al?"

"Allie is a nickname," she said. "Short for Alexandria."

"Not Alex?"

"A couple of people call me that. Mostly, just Allie." She paused a moment, laughed again. "And now, Al."

It felt pretty damn cozy. Sitting close together in the dark. Him, giving her a new nickname. Her, pleased with it.

Except it was a false intimacy. He was lying to her. She didn't even know his real name. *Jelly beans and jawbreakers.* Why had he met her while he was undercover? He could really like this woman.

"So the cancer," he prompted. "It's in remission?"

"Better than that." Her voice was a beehive, humming with happy honey.

"Meaning?"

"It's gone completely."

"I don't understand."

"Neither did the doctors." She laughed. If there *were* such things as unicorns, they would sound like Allie, full of glee and sparkly light. "When I was first diagnosed, the doctors ran a battery of tests. Told my parents to brace for a long, protracted ordeal—chemotherapy, radiation, bone marrow transplants—lasting months, years."

"I can't imagine how hard that was on them. And you."

"My parents were destroyed," she admitted. "And in an emotional tailspin. They got a second opinion. And a third. Then they wrangled an appointment at the Mayo Clinic, but it took six weeks to get in."

"And you?" he asked, hearing his voice thicken, felt his gut constrict. "How did you take the news?"

"I decided it wasn't true," she said with so much optimism and spunk it sank a knife in the center of his heart. "I imagined myself happy and healthy and whole. I cut out pictures from magazines of all the things I intended on doing with my life and pinned them to a corkboard in my bedroom. Every night before I went to sleep I would whisper over and over, *Cancer free, cancer free, nothing bad can come to me.*"

"Wow," he said, stunned by her ingenuity. "Who taught you to do those things?"

"My inner Voice," she said.

He couldn't see her face, but he could feel her smiling into the darkness and that tugged at his heartstrings.

"That's why I trust the Voice so implicitly."

"After all the chemo and radiation and bone marrow transplants, the cancer vanished?"

"That's just the thing," she said. "I never had to have any treatment. By the time we arrived at our appointment at the Mayo Clinic, there was no evidence of cancer. I'd had a spontaneous healing. Everyone's minds were boggled. But even though the medical establishment can't explain it, spontaneous regression does happen in one out of every one hundred thousand cancers or so, although they don't know how or why."

Stunned, Kade sat there absorbing the story. After a moment, he said, "I'm glad you were one of the lucky ones."

"Me too. Thing is my parents never really trusted that the cancer was gone for good. My mom's mother died of inflammatory breast cancer when mom was twelve, and she has a real fear she's going to lose me to cancer. She coddles me. I understand, and I love her to pieces, but sometimes . . . well, I'm afraid it's stunted me a tiny bit."

"How tiny?" he asked.

She laughed, bright as roses in winter. "Not very. I just moved away from home for the first time and I'm almost twenty-four. Unfortunately, my roommate moved in with her fiancé after they got engaged last week, and I need to find a new roommate soon or I'll have to move back home. I'm hoping this new job will tide me over until I can either get a permanent position somewhere or find another roommate."

"Not that I'm defending your mother's overprotectiveness, but given your history, I can see why she's having a hard time letting go, and why you are so . . ." He trailed off.

"So what?" she prodded.

"Never mind." He shouldn't have started this. Why had he said that?

"No, really, go ahead. You won't hurt my feelings. Why I am so . . . what?"

"Sweet, innocent, trusting."

"You don't know me well enough to make those assumptions," she said.

"Granted, but you asked."

"Thank you for your honesty, even though I think you're off base. Although I admit it's not the first time I've been accused of being too trusting. But that's okay. I've got faith enough for both of us."

What did she mean? Was she insinuating he had trust issues? Okay, yeah, he did have a few trust issues. Nature of the beast. He was a cop. He knew firsthand what an ugly place the world could be.

Her hair was trailing over his bare arm, tickling his skin. God, she was driving him insane and she didn't even know it.

"Um," she said. "That came out wrong. I didn't mean for it to sound like I could supply your faith for you. I can't supply anything for you. I mean, we barely know each other. It's not like we're dating or anything. We're just neighbors. We're—"

"Attracted to each other."

She gulped audibly, slid her hand from his. He

couldn't see her face, but he could feel her bend her legs to her chest and sink her head to her knees. "Yes."

"It's been a long time since I've felt anything this potent," he confessed, then clamped his jaw closed. Dammit! He shouldn't have told the truth. Should have just kept his big mouth shut. Honesty was not always the best policy.

"How long?" she whispered.

"Never," he admitted. *Shut up, dill weed!*

"Me, either," she said.

The next thing he knew, she was in his lap. He couldn't say for sure whether he'd pulled her there or if she'd jumped into his lap, but there she was. His arms went around her waist and her arms went around his neck, and he kissed her, or she kissed him, or it was some kind of cosmic, simultaneous kiss.

The universe yanking them together like magnetic kissing dolls.

The universe?

Oh, Christ. What had she done to him? He did not resist because *holy shit*, her lips were warm and soft and moist and tasted like sugar-dusted strawberries—red and ripe and rich. She was in it to win it, BASE jumping from Mount Everest and dragging him along with her.

His palms slipped under the hem of her blouse, fingers splaying over her bare back. She parted her lips and their tongues rushed to greet each other and they drank each other up.

He forgot they were in an elevator in the middle of a

blackout. He forgot he was an undercover cop and she was a suspect. He damn near forgot his own name. He was going down for the count. It was a face-plant, white-flag, full-surrender, take-me-prisoner, I'll-talk, I'll-spill, I'll-give-it -all-up-for-you-Al, knock down.

Time exploded. Shattered into a billion little fragments. Ceased to exist.

The world was her mouth, and her mouth was the world.

Her fingers combed through his hair. He cupped her face between his palms, held her gently in place while they explored this new and exciting terrain. His blood was lava, coursing through his veins, free-flowing and glowing red-hot. He eased her down onto her back, cradled her head, straddled her.

Elevator, man. Can't do this. You're in an elevator. She deserves better.

He straightened.

She moaned, gasping for air.

Lights came on. Bathing them in harsh yellow. The lift jerked upward.

They stared into each other's eyes. Her blouse had come unbuttoned. Her hair was mussed. Her lips reddened, swollen. Her eyes wide and filled with magic.

His heart knocked, full-on angry-fists-on-door-let-me-in-at-two-a.m. hammered.

Kade felt the earth shift in some fundamental way. Felt his molecules split, scramble, reorganize.

If the lift hadn't chugged to a stop . . . If the doors hadn't clanged open . . . If the apartment complex maintenance man hadn't been standing there . . .

Kade couldn't have said for sure what would have happened next.

Chapter Six

ALLIE COULDN'T GET the kiss out of her mind.

Technically, it wasn't just *a* kiss, but a series of parted lips, excited tongues, full-mouth assaults on each other. Whatever you wanted to call it, that thing they'd done in the lift, well . . . it had been her undoing.

And she couldn't quite figure out if he'd broken her or saved her.

Maybe both.

Either way, she moved through the days leading up to the Fourth of July weekend in a hazy daze of delight and excitement. She couldn't help feeling something big was unfolding, but life had taught her to stay in the present moment and to keep her mind fixed on gratitude. No matter how things were going to end between them, she was grateful for what they'd already shared.

What they were sharing . . .

Because they saw each other every day. They timed their lunch breaks to coincide—his idea—and he insisted on coming back to the town square every evening after his shift to walk her home.

Which was extremely sweet.

But her schedule was jam-packed, so they agreed that dating would have to take the back burner until after the Fourth of July, when everything calmed down.

Until then, the time they had together was limited. Whenever they were with each other, they didn't talk much. Rather, on their lunch breaks, they'd often skip food entirely, slip into a cool public building, find a secluded alcove, and kiss up a storm. On their hand-holding walks back to their apartment complex at night, Rick would ask her about her job at the popup. She loved talking about art, and she'd get carried away with the details of her work, but he seemed fascinated.

But whenever she tried to ask questions about his life, he seemed to always lead the conversation back to her.

At first, she loved the attention, but after a few days, she started to wonder if maybe he was hiding something from her. A thousand doubts popped into her head. What if he was married? What if he had a criminal record? What if he was a con man trying to run a scam on her?

Call her naive, but she didn't want to believe any of that, so she chose to think instead he was a humble, unassuming guy who simply didn't like talking about himself.

What she knew of him was scant. Mostly surface stuff. He liked chili mac, the Texas Rangers, Lone Star beer, homemade peach ice cream, 1950s film noir, and bluegrass music. He'd lost a front tooth when he was ten in a Little League accident and had a dental implant. He'd never learned how to ride a bicycle because he'd grown up riding horses. He preferred winter to summer, baseball to football, and Wranglers to Levi's.

One thing she knew for sure, he was a damn fine kisser, and she couldn't get enough of that manly mouth.

Job-wise, things were going well. The popup had opened, and Allie spent her days leading guided tours of the art gallery and relishing using her knowledge. In the mornings, before she went to work at the Visitors Center, she ran errands for Dr. Thorn, most of which entailed ferrying packages to and from the museum district in Fort Worth.

Dr. Thorn had taken her under his wing, much to Ennui's displeasure, and taught her the ins and outs of his popup business model, reiterating that he might hire her once the exhibit was over if she did a good job.

Allie found herself daydreaming about the possibilities of such an exciting career opportunity, touring from city to city, setting up popup galleries, getting people excited about art, working in her chosen field, learning, growing, creating.

But if she got offered a permanent job, that would mean leaving behind Twilight, her family and friends, and her budding relationship with Rick.

Cross that bridge when you come to it, she reminded herself. Life unfolded day by day, moment by moment, and right now, hers was unfolding spectacularly.

On Friday, Rick showed up to take her home in his freshly washed and vacuumed silver Ford pickup truck with an extended cab and running boards.

"What's this?" she asked as he opened the passenger door and helped her inside.

"I'm taking you to dinner," he said. "This will be our last chance to see each other until after the Fourth."

He was right. No more lunch-hour getaways. Twilight was expecting an influx of ten thousand tourists for the long holiday weekend, and it was all hands on deck.

It saddened her a bit that they would no longer be stealing lunch-hour kisses. But, on the bright side, they were going out for a late dinner, which was a step forward in their relationship.

"What do you have in mind?" she asked, buckling her seat belt as he started the engine, her pulse pounding a swift rat-a-tat-tat.

"Froggy's Diner is open until one a.m. in the summer," he said. "And they have killer burgers. Is that okay with you?"

"Sure." She smiled, just happy to be with him. She didn't care what or where they ate, the company was the thing.

"Are you always so easy to get along with?" he asked.

"For the most part," she said. "I'm just happy to be here."

"I like that about you, Rosy," he said.

"Rosy?" she asked. "A new nickname?"

He canted his head, glanced over at her. "Because you see the world through those beautiful rose-colored glasses."

"Is that a bad thing?"

"I dunno." He shrugged. "I worry about you."

"Why is that?"

"People can take advantage."

"Not all people. Not always. And I can't live my life worried about who is trying to take advantage of me."

His hands tightened on the steering wheel and he bit his bottom lip. She could tell he wanted to say something but was holding back.

"What?" she prodded.

"Nothing. You are who you are."

She studied his profile, the stubble at his jaw, the way his hair curled around the top of his ear, the set of his lips. "Rick?"

He turned his head again and looked at her with such compassion it took her breath. For a tough cowboy, underneath lurked a surprisingly gentle side. "Yes?"

"How hungry are you?"

He lifted a casual shoulder as if to say he could eat or not. "What do you have in mind?"

She reached across the seat, touched his knee, scared and excited by her boldness. This was a first for her. She'd never propositioned a man before. "What if we skipped the burgers and went to your place instead?"

FUELED BY TESTOSTERONE, lust, and intriguing possibilities, Kade made an immediate U-turn, propelled his Ford dually ten miles over the posted speed limit, and considered making it twenty. One flash of his badge would get him out of a ticket if he got pulled over, but he couldn't afford to tip his hand.

Yet.

While he was certain, after spending time with Allie, that she wasn't intentionally involved with the art-theft ring, he knew Thorn was using her. Setting her up to take the fall for the stolen painting. Day by day, he'd been drawing information from her about Thorn, and the more she told him, the more certain he was that she was Thorn's pasty. Then a startling thought seized him.

Ah, shit. He was using her too.

A rueful prickle of heat burned up the back of his neck. *Call it off. Take her home. Tell her this wasn't—*

She reached across the seat, rested her hand on his thigh, and whispered, "Hurry."

That one insistent, urgent word spurred him. So much for gallantry, so much for self-control.

Except he *wasn't* that guy. He prided himself on being the calm one, the cool one. The one who, while he enjoyed sex as much as the next guy, certainly never let it hijack his common sense. But damn if his hands weren't trembling as he raced around the pickup to help her out.

She launched herself into his arms, wrapped her legs around his waist and her arms around his neck. Crushing his mouth on hers, he kissed her with hot, hard desperation. Was he losing his ever-loving mind?

A happy noise oozed from her and she slipped her tongue between his teeth, catching him so off guard he staggered into the shrubbery that lined the walkway.

Blindly, he waltzed her up the flagstone pavers, clutching her tight, holding her close—kissing, kissing, kissing the sweetest mouth he'd ever tasted. Tupelo honey and state fair cotton candy and purple Pixy-Stix had nothing on his Rosy.

They stumbled into the lift together and Kade wasn't really sure how they made it to his front door without mishap. He set her down behind him and fished in his pocket for his house keys. She slid her arm around his waist and nestled her head against his back, letting him know she was all in.

He fumbled with the keys, as raw and randy as a sixteen-year-old getting laid for the first time. It niggled him, this lack of restraint, but not enough to stop. The door wrenched open and they tumbled inside.

Allie pulled his head down for another searing kiss. He tugged her up tight against his body and she raked her fingers through his hair, sending heat bullets straight to his groin.

God, he could eat her right up.

Apparently, she was thinking the same thing. She captured his bottom lip between her teeth and sucked as if she planned on devouring him whole. This blasted heat wave must have melted both the polar ice caps and the brakes on his libido.

He was a goner.

But she was too—letting go, shedding inhibitions, sighing with reckless abandon and unabashed delight.

A random thought occurred to him that struck solid and true. This headlong heedlessness was a first for her, and that revved his engines higher, hotter, spinning him out of control.

"Wait," he panted, breaking her hold on his neck, setting her aside.

"What?" she asked, sounding grumpy, frazzled.

"I gotta ask. Are you sure this is really what you want?"

Her eyes narrowed, but her pupils were wide and bright, her lips glistening with moisture. Her tousled hair fell across her cheek. Gorgeous. She was freaking gorgeous.

"I've never wanted anything more in my life." Her voice was adamant, militant.

He growled low and fierce, yanked her back into his arms. She startled, hitched in a swift breath. He loosened his hold. "Didn't mean to scare you."

"You didn't." She shook her head, eyes sparkling. "I like roller coasters."

He arched an eyebrow.

"You know, how they jerk you up, drop you down, and take your breath away." Her breathing was shallow now, and fast. As fast as his thudding pulse.

He tightened his hand on her arm, murmured, "You want a wild ride, Rosy?"

She nodded, her gaze focused on him, full of fire and energy.

"Tell me what you want, how you want it, where you want it, and I will make it happen." Promises. He was making big promises. Could he keep them?

"I like it when you're forceful," she murmured. "I'm tired of kid gloves."

Holy freaking cow, yes! Yes! "I like it when you're forceful right back," he countered.

"Good," she said. "Let's play."

He picked her up and she wrapped her legs around his waist again. He bent his knee, jammed it against the wall. She slid down his thigh until her back was pressed against the plaster, speared between his legs.

The pulse at the hollow of her throat jumped crazily.

Kade dipped his head to her neck, nibbled the throbbing vein, felt the heat and tasted her salty skin.

Allie tossed her head back, her soft blond hair falling like satin over his arm. The rough moan rolling from her throat shot through him like a steel rod, zooming straight to his shaft. His erection swelled against his zipper, desperate, insistent.

Had he ever in his life been this hard?

His hands skated up from her waist to her breasts, felt the warm, soft flesh through the thin silk of her dress as it filled his palms. Naked. He had to get her naked. How the hell did he get her out of this getup?

Did it have a zipper? Buttons? Did the dress pull right over her head? For the life of him, he couldn't seem to figure it out.

Shuddering, she thrust her breasts against his palms, her nipples knotted tight. Dear Lord, but the woman was so sexy and responsive. Every touch, every glance, every sigh was a swift arrow to his gut.

Gut, hell. He felt her everywhere—on his thigh, against his hands, in his heart.

He wanted her to feel him in the same way. Ached to know what made her writhe and squirm, whisper and groan. He craved to know her in the most intimate way possible. To lick and taste, knead and caress, bind and release. To wring her inside out until she gave him everything, had nothing left to surrender.

All of her.

He wanted all of her.

An impatient sound grated gritty across her lips and she was kissing him again, a long, deep, throaty kiss, full of heat and tongue. A kiss that turned his knees wobbly and sent his blood galloping through his body.

"Take me," she whimpered. "Take me now."

His hands ached to rip the dress right off her body. Strip off her panties. Take her forcefully, powerfully. Yes. But he didn't want to wreck her clothes or risk hurting her or scare her in any way. She indicated she wanted things rough and wooly, but oddly, surprisingly, Kade was no longer sure that was what *he* wanted.

Allie was unique. Special.

Gently, he eased her down the wall, settled her on the floor. "Not yet," he said. "I want this to last."

Mutely, she nodded, reached down to undo the buckles on the straps of her high-heeled sandals. She eased off the shoes, lost three inches of height, held them in one hand, gave him a look that was both confident and unguarded. She was so open, frighteningly so. Her enticing combination of strength and fragility stirred him. He'd never met anyone so self-assured in her vulnerability.

She spread her arms as if to say, *Take me as I am*. "Do you have any . . ." She swallowed visibly. "Um . . . protection?"

"I've got condoms." He swept her into his arms and whisked her down the hall to his bedroom, happy as hell the housekeeper had been there the day before. The place smelled like lemon air freshener and sandalwood soap.

Allie hesitated at the door to his bedroom.

He reached around to turn on the light. "Second thoughts?" he asked, sensing a change in the energy.

"No." She shook her head vigorously. "But we've been dancing. A shower maybe?"

He brought her into his embrace, dropped his head to her hair, and inhaled deeply. "I love your smell."

She tensed.

It occurred to him that maybe he shouldn't have used the word "love," but he did love her scent. It reminded him of summers spent at his grandparents' farm. She smelled like long lazy days at the swimming hole, like the white-yellow flowers that grew along the fencerow, like the chilled watermelon slices eaten on the backyard picnic table and Granny's home-churned peach ice cream.

And she smelled like gorgeous sexy woman. Never a bad thing.

Allie wrinkled her nose. "I stink like sweat."

"Maybe I like sweaty." He lowered his voice and his eyelids, giving her a sultry once-over. "Besides, we're just going to get sweatier."

She laughed, a hearty sound that illuminated his world. "You make a good point."

Kade kissed her again because he'd gone too long without the taste of her lips and whispered, "How in the hell do we get you out of that dress?"

Chapter Seven

HOLDING HER BREATH, Allie turned around so that Rick could open the buttons at the back of her dress. Normally, she wouldn't bother undoing the buttons, and would just pull the dress over her head, but she needed to feel his fingers against her back. Wanted to linger on the act of getting undressed.

Plus, for some reason, it felt safer having him at her back.

Minutes before, when he had her up against the wall and his big thigh jutted between her legs, all she'd wanted was for him to rip her clothes off and take her right there in his foyer.

Now, common sense returned along with the butterflies flapping around in her tummy. As his fingers worked the buttons, one by one, sliding lower and lower, the air hitting her bare back, revealing first her black lace bra and then her thong panties, she felt more and more exposed.

The urge to run pushed through her, although she wasn't completely sure why. She liked him. She liked him a lot. It had been a long time since she'd had sex, and, well, her body was revved and ready.

But was she?

Having sex with someone for the first time was fraught with excitement, anticipation, and, let's face it, anxiety. So many worries. So many fears.

What if he didn't like the way she looked naked? She wasn't a supermodel. Things jiggled in places they probably shouldn't. What if he had a micropenis? Conversely, what if he had a huge penis and she couldn't handle it? What if he disappointed her? What if she disappointed him? What if the sex was terrific and they wanted to do this again and again? What would that mean? Just sex or something more? Did she want something more? Was she ready for a relationship? Was he? What if Thorn gave her a permanent job and she had to move? Could they make a go of a long-distance relationship?

Cart. Horse. She was getting ahead of herself.

Calm down. Faith meant knowing everything would work out the way it was supposed to. *Breathe. Trust.*

Her mantra. Her motto. Her life metaphor.

"Do you trust me?" he whispered.

"Yes." She didn't hesitate. Everything inside Allie told her that she could trust this man.

"Because you trust everyone?"

Helpless, she smiled. What could she say? "It's worked for me so far. I've discovered that people are essentially good at heart, even the ones who don't really want to be good."

"Discernment." He shook his head. "You need it if you ever hope to achieve real independence. As long as you keep peering at the world through those rose-colored glasses, your parents are going to hover. They don't believe you can look after yourself because they *know* there are wolves in the woods."

A shiver shot through her. "Are you saying you're a wolf?"

"I'm saying you trust blindly, Rosy. You assume everyone is as nice as you are. Believe me, Al, they aren't. You have to be careful out there."

"Like you are?" she asked. "So skeptical and wary you can't ever let your guard down?"

"Maybe that's why I'm so drawn to you," he said. "I'm envious of your positive bright light."

She felt a powerful shift in the region of her heart. He was being honest and authentic. She could see it in his eyes. Hear it in his voice. Her fear evaporated.

"Allie," he whispered and undid the last button.

Her dress fell to the floor, floated around her feet. It was only then she realized she was still holding her sandals, and she let them drop to the floor.

He let out a long, low whistle.

"What is it?" she whispered, afraid to turn around to face him.

"Allie Grainger, you're the hottest damn thing I've ever laid eyes on."

She smiled to herself. Yes, okay, it was a smirk. Who wouldn't smirk when a man as incredibly handsome as Rick was making her feel as if she was the most gorgeous creature on the planet?

"You are . . ." He pushed his hair off his forehead, blew out his breath through pursed lips. "I am the luckiest . . . well, wow."

He stepped closer, turned her around, and framed her face with his big palms, tilting her face up. Any lingering doubts swimming around in her head evaporated as his hand slipped from her face to her shoulders and the sultry light in his eyes said, *Everything is gonna be just fine, darlin'.*

"Your turn." She reached for his shirt, worked the buttons with frantic fingers.

"Slow down," he whispered and tugged her closer, his palms gliding over her waist, past her hips, moving around to cup her butt. "We've got all night."

Allie drew in a long, hungry breath through her teeth as if sucking air through a straw. "I want to . . ."

He grinned and ran his fiery tongue along her collarbone, detonating an earthquake of tiny shivers over her body. "What?"

Groaning, she rested her brow against the top of his

head and threaded her fingers through his hair. "I've gotta see you without that damned shirt on."

A chuckle rumbled up through his lungs, sounding lively and lived-in. "All right, all right."

He stepped back and did a little striptease, unbuttoning his shirt one button at a time. He coyly gave her a flash of flesh, then pulled the edges of his western shirt together, hiding his chest for a second, before going on to the next button.

"Devil," she muttered and reached to help him, but he playfully swatted her away.

"Hands to yourself, missy," he said, but quickly polished off the last button and pulled the hem from his waistband, stripped the shirt off his shoulders, and flung it to the floor beside her dress.

What a view! Allie broke out in a sweat. Crank up the air conditioner! Call the fire department! There was a five-alarm fire in her undies.

She couldn't help staring, her gaze transfixed, tracing every muscle with her eyes, and licking her lips, her imagination exploding with possibilities. He was beyond movie-star quality. Beyond beach body. He was a frigging work of art. Honestly, the guy was so fantastically ripped, he could have been a cyborg.

Hmm. Her gaze dipped to the lovely V area that slipped into the waistband of his low-slung jeans. Maybe he *was* a cyborg.

Unlike most guys his age, he was not pierced or inked. Nothing colored or punctured the perfection that was Rick Braedon. He was pure. Pristine. Nature in the raw. There was no need for adornment or embellishment when a man looked this good. Ink or piercings would only detract.

Allie couldn't help herself. She splayed her palm over his heart, sighed helplessly at the durable feel of his muscles beneath her skin. She wanted to ask him how many hours a day it took to stay in tip-top shape, but his thumb hooked her chin and he was angling her mouth up for another kiss and she forgot about everything except the sheer pleasure of being with him. Small talk took the back burner.

His long, broad, tanned fingers got busy with the clasp on her bra, working the hook-and-eye system with breath-stealing adeptness.

Boldly, Allie reached for the snap of his jeans.

He grunted, a surprised sound, laced with delight, and she smiled as his lips closed over hers with fresh urgency.

She undid the snap, reached for the zipper, felt the pressure of his hard heat against her fingers. Commando. He was going commando, his bare flesh velvet steel.

Simultaneously, they sucked in air. His eyes darkened, and she felt hers widen. "Mmm," he said.

Every muscle in her body tightened, clenched. Need sliced through her like a chef's knife, sharp and deft. She forgot to exhale, the craving almost too much to handle. She wasn't wildly experienced sexually—she'd had three lovers in her twenty-four years—but she couldn't recall ever feeling this level of mind-bending desire.

Rick's mouth moved from her lips to her chin, underneath her jaw to the hollow of her throat, taking his time with the leisurely trip. His hand whisked off her bra and his head dipped to curl his blistering tongue around her nipple.

She grasped his shoulders and throbbing energy surged from his body into her palms, shot straight through her arms, pulsing down, down, down to end where she was melting, moist and needy.

Chuckling, he shifted from the first damp, peaked nipple to the second, until she squirmed, desperate and mewling.

She was so charged up, she barely noticed he'd been gradually waltzing her into his bedroom. She blinked at the big king-sized bed, fuzzy-headed but thrilled to be there. The room smelled of him, masculine and provocative. He danced her to the foot of the bed and gently tipped her over.

Her butt landed on the edge of the mattress and she raised her knees to scoot up farther, but he pressed a hand against her hip, stopping her. "I've got you right where I want you," he said, his words throaty and mysterious.

She shuddered, but it was a good kind of shiver, hard and hopeful. She lowered her knees, her legs dangling off the bed.

"Keep your knees on the footboard," he instructed

as he knelt in front of her, and it fully hit her what he intended.

"Oh, my!" she breathed, not really meaning to say that out loud.

"Yes, ma'am." His voice was a caress, heavy and slow, and he hooked his thumbs in the elastic band of her panties.

He edged the scrap of black silk down her legs, eased it over her knees, slipped it from her heels, first one side and then the other. He tossed the panties over his shoulder with a cavalier flick of his wrist and a wolfish smile on his face.

Nervously, she pressed her knees together. Her doubts and fears galloping back. Did she really want to go through with—?

He tenderly parted her knees and ran his fingers over her inner thighs as if he was playing heavenly music on a keyboard. Any and all thoughts fled her mind as total awareness and heightened sensation claimed her.

Those incredible lips of his pressed hot, fervent kisses up the inside of her leg, inching closer and closer to her feminine core.

"Do you like this?" he murmured. "Do you want more?"

"Yesss," she hissed through clenched teeth. "Yesss, yesss, yesss." A sublime snake of yeses. A streaming steam of yeses. A never-ending circle. Yes-yes-yes-yes.

The closer he got to her entrance, the tighter her muscles tensed. By the time his tongue touched her most sensitive area, her fists were clenched, her eyes squeezed closed, her entire body stiff as a drum skin, her breath coming in short, gulping staggers.

"Relax," he murmured against her skin, sending a sweet vibration buzzing through her.

Yeah, like that was so easy when he was doing the most incredible things to her. She gasped and arched her back against his wicked, eager tongue. Heat and moisture. Sensation layered on top of sensation. She couldn't think. Couldn't breathe. All she could do was surrender to this man and his amazing bedroom skills. He knew what he was doing.

A couple of her boyfriends had tried oral sex before, but it had never been like this. Those instances had been half-hearted at best, uncomfortable at worst, until Allie had started to believe she didn't really like it.

Rick put an end to that silly misguided belief.

He took his time, as if savoring the world's most sumptuous meal. He had her giggling and gasping, panting and praying, clutching his head and crying for more. The man was a clit magician. The clitoris whisperer.

His fingers slid into the game, stretching and teasing, ticking things up another notch. She had no idea there were so many levels of arousal. How was this even possible?

She felt like a rosebud blossoming in the heat of a nurturing sun, opening up, flowering wild and free, blooming to her full potential. She was a nymph, a goddess, a queen.

Hell, she was a glistening, glittering galaxy!

Time hung suspended. In amber. In honey. In treacle. Languid and warm and rare. A golden moment that stretched out limitlessly, teasing her with the thought that this was how the universe secretly existed. In the immutable vastness of *now*.

It seemed fated. As if from that moment when he'd saved her from those stampeding longhorns and later when he'd tucked her in the crook of his arm in the elevator, they'd been building toward this encounter.

Toward each other.

His touch, his skill, his confidence pushed her closer and closer to the edge. Sensation built, grew, swelled. Pushed down on her. Pressure. Heat. Vibration.

Not already. Not yet. She wanted more. Needed to slow things down.

"Please," she whispered. "No."

"Am I hurting you?" His hand stilled, his voice filled with concern.

"Not at all. I'm just . . . It's just . . . I'm not ready. I want this to last."

"Ah, Rosy." He laughed, kindness in his chuckle. "This is only the beginning. The first of many."

Her heart did a trippy little hope tap—tat-tat-tatty-tat-tat. Did he mean the first of many orgasms? Or the first of many nights like tonight?

She sneaked a peek at his face, gazing down between her knees. His naughty lips, curled into a naughty smile, glistened wetly in the muted light. He looked smug and so damn handsome she didn't know if she could survive many more nights like this one.

"I want you to have fun too," she said.

"Believe me, darlin'," he drawled. "I'm having the time of my life."

"Doesn't—?"

"It's okay. Just let yourself go."

She was about to protest that it wasn't fair for her to get her jollies while he still had his jeans on, but he lowered his head and went back to doing what he did so masterfully.

That amazing mouth burning her, branding her, banishing her to the outer reaches of reason. Her body was alive with electricity. Tingling, throbbing, tickling. Jolt after jolt of sensation hit her. Robbed her of thought. And rationality.

She was an animal. Wild. Hungry. Desperate.

"Rick," she shouted, not even aware she was calling his name. "Rick!" A punctuation. "Rick, Rick, Rick." A chant. Maybe it should be her new mantra. In this moment, he was her hope, her faith, her everything. "Rick, Rick, Rick, Rick."

His hands and tongue performed wily wizardry, provoked, pandered.

She arched her back off the mattress, her fingers latching on to his hair and not letting go. She cried out, a mad, tumultuous sound, full-bodied and braggy. Hopefully, his apartment had thick walls. The growing heat flared, flamed, consuming her in rhythmic waves of vivid yellow starbursts.

He slowed.

Teasing.

"More," she whispered between adrenaline-fueled giggles. "Please more."

He was fully in charge. She was at his mercy. But while he teased, he didn't torment. Not much anyway. Just enough to make things even more pleasurable. He knew how to walk the fine line between pleasure and pain. Escalating the tension. Holding back in order to push her into more demanding heights.

Allie didn't fight it. Just let him take control. Allowed him to blow her away. To cast his magic spell. Body. Mind. Soul.

Five seconds into the no-holds-barred onslaught and Allie was fairly certain she was going to pass out if something didn't give soon.

And then, oh God, she was gone. So gone. Disappeared. Vanished. She gasped, grasped, panted, quivered. Transformed from regular old Allie Grainger, Visitors Center receptionist and popup art gallery temporary assistant into a high priest. Venus. Aphrodite. Clíodhna. One of those incredible goddesses.

Whimpering, she clutched a pillow to her chest, trying to absorb what just happened. He kicked off his cowboy boots, shucked off his pants.

She gave him a long look, devoured him with her

eyes. Sighed. If she keeled over of a heart attack right now, she'd die happy. She spread her legs wider. Motioned him with come-hither fingers.

He climbed onto the mattress between her splayed legs, watched her with narrowed, inquisitive brown eyes.

It had been a long time since she'd had such a powerful orgasm. Actually, she couldn't even remember ever having an orgasm that earth-shaking, soul-stirring, world-rocking. And, greedy girl that she was, Allie wanted more. No, not just wanted more. She craved it with a yearning so strong, it rattled her to the core.

Rick seemed to be on the same page. He paused to dig a foil packet from the pocket of his jeans. With practiced expertise, he had the condom open and rolled on in under eight seconds.

He paused, his eyes searching her face. "How are you doing, sweetheart?"

Sweetheart.

A squishy feeling squeezed her chest. It was a dangerous word that conjured boyfriend images. Yes, she liked him. Yes, this was a very good night. Yes, she wanted more, but she didn't expect it. Or, rather, didn't want to start expecting it.

Sweetheart stirred expectations, and expectations stirred fear.

"Allie?"

"Fine." She bobbed her head, then realized he was checking to make sure she was ready to take this show to its final conclusion. "I'm fine. Finer than fine."

He stretched out beside her, raised up on one elbow, and looked down at her with an expression of such acceptance and tenderness that her heart floated up out of her chest and into her throat, bobbing like a helium-filled balloon.

Remember this: balloons burst. Or float away. They don't stay bright and cheery and high forever.

He leaned toward her, his big body parallel to hers. "Is it okay if I kiss you now?"

"You don't have to ask permission," she said. "I want this as much as you do."

"Allie." He said her name simply and gathered her against him. Inhaled the scent of her hair. Pressed his mouth against hers.

He tasted of her. Salty and sexy. What a turn-on!

She tugged his head down, deepening the kiss. Letting him know it was okay to share. She loved the mingling, the merging, the magic of two people fully enjoying each other's bodies.

"Mmm," he moaned as if tasting the most fabulous meal ever cooked.

They laughed together. And kissed. Long and slow and creatively.

He rolled her over, flipping her on top of him, her knees falling to either side of his hips, straddling him. His hands circled her waist, holding her poised over this straining erection.

"Look at me," he whispered.

They exchanged glances.

"Do you feel it?" he asked.

"What?" she whispered back.

"Our energies converging."

Oh, boy, did she feel it! The heat and vibration surging from him into her even without yet being joined.

Slowly, he began to lower her down onto him. She reached to touch his shaft, to guide him into her willing wetness.

"No hands," he commanded. "Let our bodies find their way."

His control was amazing. Millimeter by millimeter, he lowered her until she could feel the throbbing head of him pulsating at her entrance. Full of vital life force. She wanted to engulf him. Absorb him. Be part of him.

She wriggled, trying to get lower, trying to connect even more with him. But his hands held firmly around her waist, holding her at that exquisite level of almost having what she wanted, but not quite able to get there.

"Bastard," she said, and he laughed.

But in a moment, he relinquished and eased her down on top of him. She gasped, joyous. He grinned and patted her butt as she settled in, her body stretching over his.

She shifted, savoring the pressure of his body inside hers. He hissed a you-feel-so-damn-good sound that vibrated throughout her body. Shivers of pleasure washed over her.

They were fully connected. No separation. Allie and this man she barely knew; the man who'd saved her twice.

She stared down at him and he peered up at her, and for a sweet, blissful moment they didn't move. Then he cupped her breasts and she rocked forward and he groaned.

I might never see him again. The notion rolled around in her head. Of course she would see him again. They lived in the same building. They worked in the same area. If she wanted to get real about it, what she meant was, *I might not ever get to do this with him again.*

Pinch. Twist. Ah, yes. The truth.

Her heart skipped a beat. Was this a one-night stand? She'd been swept away by need and desire. Hadn't really thought this through. How did she feel about that?

Rick pulled her head down and kissed her thoroughly. A kiss that seemed to promise they would do this again and again and again.

The look in his eyes, the emotions gripping her when he held her gaze for so long, told her this was more than a casual thing. This was a relationship. It might only be a physical relationship, but they were together. Maybe not forever, maybe not for very long, but they were coupled.

Joined.

Merged.

Like it or not, this night meant something. The paradigm had shifted, and the way she thought about sex would never be the same. She was changing. He was changing her. From a girl who looked through rose-colored glasses at the world, to a woman who could see clearly the beauty in faults and flaws as well as strengths and assets.

Life wasn't about ignoring the problems and hoping for the best. Rather, she was growing in the knowledge that seeing those problems as opportunities and tackling them with her eyes wide open made her stronger, tougher, and more independent. She didn't need anyone to save her.

She could save herself.

If this relationship crashed and burned, losing him would not destroy her. She could and would handle it.

But right now, she was going to handle *him*. In the best way possible. Allie smiled in the darkness.

"What's so funny?" he asked.

"You," she said, reaching around to grip his hips and pull herself down farther onto him.

"Woman," he gasped and sunk his fingers into her buttocks. "You're driving me out of my ever-loving mind."

She rocked back and forth, giggling.

"Ride 'em, cowgirl," he said, wrapping his arms around her back and sitting up, sending her somehow impossibly deeper. He fisted one hand around her hair, holding her in place while he captured her lips and kissed her hard and long.

They were rocking together now. A single unit. Bouncing on the mattress, squeaking the bedsprings.

Drunk with the wildness of their joining, of him, of them, she closed her eyes and let the eclipse slide over her.

"That's right, sweetheart," he said, using that lovely word again. "Just let go. I've got this. I've got *you*."

His voice was a fleece blanket, warm and soft, carrying her away, keeping her safe. He nuzzled her neck, nibbled her earlobe. His tongue licked her tender flesh. Goose bumps raised on her skin, spread down her body.

Without warning, he tucked his arm around her waist and flipped them over in one smooth unit until he was on top, cradling her head in his hands, peering into her eyes.

Allie felt him grow harder inside her and she let out a little moan.

"God, you are so beautiful. I've imagined you naked in my bed from the moment I saw you walking across Main Street."

"Really?" She smiled, feeling a bit self-conscious. She never thought of herself as particularly beautiful. Pretty, okay. But beautiful? Not by a long shot.

In his eyes, she saw her reflection, and realized he truly found her beautiful. That touched her, humbled her.

Rick stroked her cheeks with his fingers, planted kisses everywhere he touched. Her forehead. Her chin. The tip of her nose. "Do you have any idea how sexy you are?"

When he said it like that, she *felt* sexy. She lowered her lashes, sent him a coy glance.

He tugged her closer to him, moved inside her. Slowly at first, getting a leisurely rhythm going. He tilted his pelvis against hers, rubbing the spot that sent electric sensation flooding her.

She surrendered. Just let go.

And what a ride!

Their mouths, their bodies, their minds. Creative. Expressive. Instruments of pleasure. But it was more than that. Higher. Rarer. Performance art. They were creating art with their bodies, with each other, a magnificent, timeless dance of love.

This was why people called it lovemaking. She felt cherished, and she cherished him in return.

But along with the cherishing came the charging heat and fiery desire. The blistering, crackling, sizzling need. They were caught in a swirl of lips and tongues, arms and legs. Tangled. Entangled. Enmeshed.

A dance of penetration and retreat. Of ebb and flow. Profound. Complex. Tricky. Sticky. Wet and willing.

Sensitive. Her entire body was hypersensitive to his touch. Receptive. She was aware of every brush of his fingers, every breath he took—the taste of his skin, the sight of his bare tanned skin, the throb of him.

Her cells tingled and glowed. It seemed a top secret message from the universe. Confidential and hush-hush. Just the two of them in on this great and powerful answer to the mystery of life.

Love.

She thought it. Felt it. And in that moment, knew it.

A breathless whirl. Visions of possibilities. Shadow and light. The world was inside of her and she was inside the world. Vast. Endless. No limits.

Falling. Oh, she was falling.

While at the same time, rising. Surging up on energy and passion. Soaring to the apex of something big. A comet shooting across the sky, high, arcing . . .

Headed for a beautiful, shattering plunge into unmapped territory.

Rick was pushing her to those majestic heights, his body thrusting into hers. She writhed beneath him, her hands fisting the sheets, toes curling in ecstasy.

"You okay, Rosy?" he whispered, his voice husky and brusque with urgency. He was as ready as she was.

"Yes, oh, yes." She pushed against him, urgent for more, ready to share the ultimate with him.

He responded. Quickened the pace, deepening the pressure, rocking into her hard and swift. The world tilted. The universe rattled. The galaxy split.

Every part of her turned electric indigo, icy hot, and fiery cold. Dichotomy. Yin and yang. Opposites forming the perfect whole.

Their sweaty bodies clinging, climbing, crashing. She cried out his name. He groaned hers.

She had never felt so magnificent. So sexy. So much like a woman.

A final thrust. That last stroke and she cracked wide open. The deep, shudder of release cleaving through the middle of her. Robbing her of breath. Sapping her strength. Draining all the tension from her body.

She sucked in a mouthful of sheet, laughed. Sighed. Cried.

Rick made noises of his own. Male, guttural, earthy.

She grinned, feeling erotic and powerful. She had reduced him to a quivering mass inside of her.

Rick fell to his side, gathered her in his arms, and cradled her in the crook of his elbow. He kissed her cheek and tightened his grip as if he intended on never letting her go.

His face was shiny in the light from the hallway, his satisfied smile so incredibly sexy she could hardly stand it. She had just made love with this strong, gorgeous man.

And it was the best night of her entire life.

Chapter Eight

DRIVEN BY THIRST, Allie padded through Rick's living room wearing nothing but his western shirt that hit at her knees. It was easier than putting on her button-up-the-back dress and besides, his smell was on the shirt and she liked it. She inhaled, grinned at the sunlight seeping in through the window blinds.

The kitchen was laid out much like her own. Small galley kitchen with top-of-the-line upgrades. Quartz countertops. White cabinets. Stainless steel appliances. Marble floor. The old apartment building had undergone major renovations with the recent gentrification of the Twilight historical district. The makeover had shot rent prices through the roof, which was why she was working two jobs until she could find a new roomie.

How did Rick afford his apartment without a roommate?

It occurred to her how little she knew about him. What did he do when he wasn't a diorama actor? Maybe he was a trust-fund baby and didn't really have to work.

The urge to snoop through his things slipped over her, but she fought against it. No. She wasn't going to violate his privacy. Some people might consider her foolish, but she trusted him. Especially after last night.

Smiling at the memory and the sweet soreness in her body, she fingered her puffy lips, dry and swollen from the force and quantity of his kisses.

Water. Yes, that was what she was after.

The kitchen was different from hers in color and content. Hers was Tuscan yellow with elaborate murals she'd painted on the walls, and it was pretty well devoid of cooking supplies. She was a takeout kind of girl. Her kitchen mostly housed her art supplies. Her previous roommate, a flight attendant, had been cool with that. The next roommate might not be so forgiving of modeling clay in the cookie jar and charcoal pencils in the pantry. She'd have to rethink the logistics of where she stored her art supplies if that happened.

Rick's walls were a trendy gray. The entire kitchen was black, white, and shades of gray. The pops of color came from food. Avocados in a crystal bowl. Bananas in a hammock. Oranges, lemons, limes, grapefruits in a big wicker basket. Lush red tomatoes on the counter.

Was he a foodie?

She opened the refrigerator and peeked in—a girl could only contain her curiosity for so long. Clean, well-organized. Grass-fed butter in the dairy drawer. Artisan cheeses. Full-fat cream. A crisper full of kale, spinach, lettuce, broccoli, carrots, and cabbage.

A foodie and healthy to boot.

But of course. A man didn't get a body like that by eating junk food.

She spied a pitcher of filtered water and took it out of the fridge. Found a glass in the cabinet, poured up the cold, clear water, and sucked down the whole glass in three thirsty gulps.

Then her eyes fell on the espresso maker. Coffee. Mmm.

It took her a few minutes to figure out the complicated machine, but she finally coaxed a cappuccino out of it. Took a sip.

Holy cowboy! That was one great cup of coffee.

Heavenly. Wrapping both hands around the oversized cup, she stepped to the window that looked out into the shared courtyard. She could see her own apartment across the way.

She loved the early-morning light. The subtle shift of colors. Sleepy pinks, purples, and blues, merging inch by inch into the soft glow of yellow and orange. She inhaled the steam of coffee, the smell of Rick, the freshness of a new day.

A rich sadness crept over her. Last night, as wonderful as it had been, was over. In the past.

And the future?

Well, that was pretty uncertain, wasn't it? She had no

idea what last night meant in terms of going forward. Things might not work out. He might not be as invested as she was.

But Allie couldn't regret last night. She'd learned a long time ago to live in the moment. Yes, sometimes that made her impulsive, but when you stayed in the moment, you could handle practically anything.

Right now, the morning was beautiful, the coffee was exquisite, her body was sore in the best possible way, and she felt well and thoroughly loved.

A tear slid down her cheek, surprising her. She swiped it away and found herself filled suddenly with a melancholy yearning she could not explain nor name.

But she wasn't upset. There was a special kind of beauty in the uncertainty. Her heart was open. Ready for what lay ahead. It was okay. She was okay. No matter what happened between her and Rick.

She turned from the window, trailed into the living room. Savored the feel of the floor beneath her feet as it shifted from marble to hardwood. From cool to warm.

This room was straightforward. Masculine. Big leather couch and chairs. A lamp made of horseshoes. Another made from an old cowboy boot. Buffalo-hide rug. A deer-antler hat rack with three Stetsons hanging from the horns. One black, one white, one straw. Cowboy staples.

Pictures of rodeo cowboys in barbwire frames lined one wall. She stepped closer to study the riders on the backs of bucking bulls. Realized it was the same cowboy in each of the ten photographs. A safety helmet shielded his face, but she recognized him.

Rick.

Except written in pencil at the bottom of each picture was the name of the bull and the rider—Kade. El Diablo and Kade, Freight Train and Kade, Tornado and Kade . . .

Allie cocked her head. Studied the pictures intimately. Did Rick have a twin brother named Kade?

"Morning, Nosy Rosy."

Caught off guard, Allie squeaked, jumped, spun around.

Rick was standing between the hallway and the living room, wearing only a pair of boxer shorts and a devastating smile. The cowlick at the back of his head stood straight up and he had an adorable sheet crease across his right cheek. "Haven't you heard? Curiosity killed the cat."

"Now you know the truth about me," she teased. "I'm not above snooping."

"Remind me to keep my secrets under lock and key," he said.

Remind me. As if there was going to be a next time. Her heart took off like a fledgling eagle, wings quivering on a stiff breeze.

"You have a brother." She nodded at the pictures. "Kade. Are you two twins?"

He came closer, but his eyes were on the pictures, and he had an odd look on his face. She wondered if he and his brother were estranged. Or if something terrible had happened to Kade.

Allie bit her bottom lip. Why couldn't she mind her own business?

"My dad raised rodeo bulls," he said.

She noticed he did not answer her question about Kade. She would not ask again. It was none of her business, and clearly, he did not want to talk about his twin.

He stepped closer, took the coffee cup from her hands, set it on the fireplace mantel above her head. Tugged her into his arms. Kissed her softly.

"There're things I can't tell you, Allie," he murmured. "Not now. Not yet. But I want you to know this, you *can* trust me."

The hairs at the back of her neck prickled at his cryptic words. But she trusted him. Yes, she did. He'd never given her reason to doubt him. She believed people lived up to your expectations of them. And she expected the best from him.

"Does your dad still raise bulls?" she asked, mainly because she didn't know what else to say.

"Dad died when I was twenty," he said.

Her throat clenched. "I'm so sorry."

His shoulders went up, a casual shrug. She'd seen him do that before. A defense mechanism against his feelings. "It was almost ten years ago. I've weathered it. We had our differences, but he was a good father. Taught me about honor and integrity. I'm grateful I had him for as long as I did."

The melancholy she'd felt in the kitchen was back, settling into her bones in a new way. She wondered how losing his father so young had changed him. It couldn't have been easy.

"Thank you," she said. "For sharing."

That shoulder lift again. Water off a duck's back. But he didn't fool her.

"So, your dad was a professional cowboy?" she said.

"No." Rick shook his head. "Raising bulls was his hobby, his passion. By profession, he was a cop."

She really didn't know what Rick did for a living. Barely knew him at all. A tiny snake of fear coiled in the bottom of her pelvis, but she pushed it aside because she didn't understand it.

"Try getting away with anything when your dad is in law enforcement," Rick said. "I got busted every single time I played hooky from school or snuck out the bedroom window to go hang out with my friends. Of course—" he wriggled his eyebrows comically "—I did learn how to do creative things with handcuffs."

"You'll have to show me that skill sometime." She laughed, but then cut if off quickly. She didn't want him to think she expected anything from him. Like a future.

"Hmm," he said, a sultry look coming into his eyes, a devilish grin yanking up the corners of his mouth. "Sounds like a fun date."

A thrill rushed through her at that look, his smile. Maybe, possibly, there was something big here. Fingers crossed. Hopes raised. Darn it. She couldn't help herself.

"Dad dreamed of retiring early, becoming a full-time rancher. He wanted to leave a legacy for me and my ..." He paused as if he had planned on saying something else, hunched his shoulders, shifted his gaze to the photographs. "Us kids. He loved to brainstorm names for the ranch. Small Wonders Ranch was his favorite because he said it would be a small wonder if it ever happened. He'd put down earnest money on some land in Jubilee the day before he was killed in the line of duty."

Allie reached for Rick's hand, interlaced her fingers through his. Felt the throb of his pulse sear through her palm. She squeezed his hand. Said nothing. What was there to say? She couldn't fix the past. Couldn't change things for him.

"Thanks," he murmured.

"For what?"

"Listening."

Allie hugged him tight. He rested his chin on the top of her head. She'd gotten a miracle in her life with the cancer. He hadn't been so lucky. "Your dad would be proud of you becoming a cowboy."

"I don't know about that," he said, tilting her face up so he could drop a kiss on her lips. "Stripping off my shirt for tourists and playacting at being a cowboy is a lot different from actually being a cowboy."

"Cowboy is as cowboy does," she quipped around the sweet pressure of his mouth. "If you do cowboy things that makes you a cowboy."

He pulled back, peered at her. "In the eyes of camera-wielding Yankee tourists, maybe."

"Cut yourself some slack."

A rueful smile claimed his face. "My dad used to say the same thing. He said I was too hard on myself."

"Smart man."

"He would have liked you." His voice held a light, wistful note.

A shaft of sunlight slipped through the partially opened blinds, casting his handsome cheeks in angular shadows. Her heart swooped, dove.

Allie sighed. "I have to go get ready for work."

"No time for breakfast?" he asked. "I make a mean frittata."

She shrugged shyly, her self-consciousness roaring back. Shook her head. The longer she stayed, the more likely it was she'd start spinning forever fantasies. She was too good at that.

"You prefer French toast?" he asked.

"No," she said. "Eggs are fine, but . . . I really can't stay."

"Why not?"

"My mom calls me every morning at seven-thirty. She'll flip if I don't answer."

"You can talk to her here," he said. "I'll leave the room. Or, you can text her and tell her that you're having breakfast with a friend and you'll call her later."

"Then she'll want to know what friend and I'm just not very good at lying."

"Your mother is all up in your business, huh?"

"Our relationship is a work in progress. I'm weaning her slowly."

"Just tell her the truth."

Allie groaned. "Then she'll want to know everything about you."

"Oh," he said, his pupils constricting to pinpricks. "I get it."

"Get what?" She cocked her head, confused.

"You're ashamed of me." He sounded hurt.

"That's not it. Not at all."

"No?"

They stood there looking at each other, and in that bath of sunlight, she saw everything that was wrong with her life. She cruised along on the current, not resisting where circumstances took her. Just floated. Surrendered. Trusted. Sometimes that was a good thing. Trusting that it was okay to let go of control had gotten her through many dark days with surprising ease. But sometimes, like now, not resisting, not having a strong opinion, not standing up for what she wanted, robbed her of her independence.

"You know what?" she said. "I think I will have that frittata."

Rick grinned and rubbed his palms together, headed for the kitchen. Allie located her purse where she'd dropped it in the foyer the night before, dug out her cell phone, and texted her mom.

Late night. Busy A.M. Call U later.

She closed her phone, feeling more powerful and liberated than she'd ever felt. This was *her* life and she was in the driver's seat.

THE CARDINAL SIN of undercover work? Sleeping with a suspect.

Last night, Kade had committed the biggest bonehead move of his career. He'd let his desire for Allie seduce him into believing it was okay to cross that line.

What had he been thinking?

That was just it. He hadn't been thinking. Now here he was, Allie looking at him with sweet eyes and expectations he couldn't fulfill.

Not as long as he was undercover, and she was working for Thorn.

Poignant regret took a bite out of him. He felt the pain as a hollow ache deep inside his heart. Not that he regretted sleeping with her. Rather, he regretted lying to her. Yes, it was his job. Yes, if he hoped to catch Thorn, he still could not come clean. The problem was, he'd jumped the gun and took her to bed before he should have, and now he had a horrible feeling he'd ruined any long-term chances he had with Allie.

Not to mention putting his promotion in jeopardy.

You screwed up, Richmond.

Was there any way to make it right?

A frittata is not going to do it.

Maybe not, but at least he could feed her, and while he did that, maybe he could nudge her to talk more about Thorn. The sooner he could nail the art thief, the sooner he could tell Allie who he was, and the sooner he could make his intentions known.

Assuming she'll still talk to you.

"Can I do anything to help?" she asked, planting her sexy little butt on the countertop.

God, she was adorable wearing his shirt.

"You're doing it."

"What's that?" She swished her legs back and forth, lightly bumping them against the cabinets.

"Looking absolutely gorgeous."

She ran a hand through her hair, lowered her lashes in a shy gesture. "Well, fiddlesticks, Mr. Braedon, you are a smooth talker."

Hell, even her sayings were cute. But it was a punch of reality to hear her call him by his alias.

"You like mushrooms, onions, and garlic?" he mumbled, wishing he could just come clean.

"Yes, please."

"Coming right up." He worked for a few minutes, sautéing the vegetables in a skillet before adding the eggs, trying to work out the best way to steer the conversation around to Thorn.

"So." He popped the frittata into the oven. "What's your work schedule like today?"

"You know I won't have time for a lunch break."

He stepped over to her. She wrapped her legs around his waist, drew him closer. "Me either. Biggest tourist weekend of the year."

"Kiss me," she said.

In for a penny, in for a pound. No putting the genie back in that bottle. He might as well take his kisses where he could get them. When she found out he'd been lying to her, using her to catch a thief, well, this might be the last kiss he ever got from her. He should make it count.

He kissed her long and slow, savoring the moment, savoring her. "No break between the Visitors Center and the popup gallery?" he asked.

"No." She shook her head. "Today is a big day. They're bringing in the Remington this morning for the start of the long weekend and security will be tight. Extra protocol to wade through, and some dignitaries are coming in for a VIP reception this afternoon. I'm actually sneaking out of the Visitors Center early to get over there and help set up."

"Dang," he said. "I was hoping to get a minute or two alone with you."

"Not until after the Fourth," she reminded him. "Dr. Thorn is on edge with the rolling blackouts, and he's terrified that if a blackout happens while the Remington is in the gallery, someone might try to steal it. He's got a backup generator, flashlights, and lanterns on hand in case the electricity goes out."

"I'm sure the Twilight PD and the Hood County Sheriff's Department have it under control," he said, feeling his muscles bunch and tighten.

"Oh, Dr. Thorn has hired his own security too," Allie said.

"He's that nervous over a rolling blackout?"

"We *have* had three this summer. The exceptional heat is taxing the AC."

What was Thorn up to? Why hire extra security if he wanted to steal the painting? Unless the "security" he was hiring was actually part of the theft ring. Mental note: check to see if Thorn hired extra security in the other places he worked and if there had been any power outages on the off chance there was more to the rolling blackouts than it seemed on the surface.

Then again, who knew? Maybe Thorn wasn't even involved. Maybe it was someone in his employ.

Like Allie?

He studied her. Soft smile. Slender, delicate fingers rolling the sleeves of his shirt up to her elbows. Mussed hair tangled about her shoulders.

No way. He didn't believe that for a second. But he was a cop. He had to at least consider the possibility.

The oven timer dinged. He grabbed the hot pad, took out the sizzling skillet.

"That smells so good." Allie leaned over his arm, inhaled deeply, her chest rising with her breath.

He dished up the frittata and they sat down at his kitchen table across from each other.

"Omigod." She moaned. "This tastes even better than it smells. Where did you learn to cook?"

"Mom believed in sexual equality. Boys should learn how to cook, and girls should learn how to maintain their cars."

"Can your twin brother, Kade, cook this well?" she asked.

Guilt was a buzz saw, cutting him up into tiny pieces. He wanted to tell her the truth, come clean about who he was and why he'd lied to her. He knew that would be the worst possible thing he could do, but, jelly beans and jawbreakers, it took everything he had in him not to do it anyway. This was dangerous territory, and he couldn't risk her asking too many questions about his "twin" and raise her suspicions.

"Do you cook?" he asked instead.

"Not like this." She shook her head, gave him the lazy smile of someone who was well and truly satisfied. "You could be on a cooking show."

He snorted, guilt making him sound a little too harsh. "No, thanks."

They fell silent. Kade pushed his eggs around on the plate. His appetite had vanished.

"May I ask you a question?" Allie asked a few minutes later, her voice coming out thin and low.

He raised his head and she stared at him as if she were trying to figure out a complicated puzzle. The corner of her bottom lip caught up between her teeth. Just a few hours ago, he'd been nibbling on that delectable lip as if he owned it.

"Depends on the question," he hedged, and braced himself for more questions about his mysterious brother.

She put down her fork, took another big inhale as if she too were bracing herself for something that could change their entire relationship. Her eyes fixed on his and there was an undercurrent of intense emotion blowing her pupils wide open, dark and unfathomable. "What's the biggest lie you've ever told?"

Oh, shit! He was busted. She knew he didn't have a twin brother. Knew he'd been lying to her. The hairs on the nape of his neck lifted, arched, and the chair seemed to melt away beneath him. His mouth was dry, his skin rippling.

"Allie, I—"

"I ask," she said, speaking so quickly her words rolled together, "because I've been living with this lie, and I don't know what to do about it. If I tell the truth, I'll lose my job at the popup, but if I don't tell the truth, and I end up getting a permanent job with Dr. Thorn . . . well . . . the lie will be this ticking time bomb just waiting to explode."

"Hold up." He blinked, not sure he was following her. "What?"

"I lied to get the job at the art gallery," she said. "Or rather, I didn't correct an erroneous perception they had about me."

"They who?"

"Dr. Thorn and Ennui."

"Ennui?" Kade scratched his head.

"Oops, sorry." Allie grinned and slapped her palm over her mouth. "She's Dr. Thorn's personal assistant. Her real name is Daphne, but she acts so bored with life, in my head, I call her Ennui."

"What was the lie?" he asked, relieved that she wasn't onto him. His mouth filled with a strange taste, metallic, bitter, salty. The taste of guilt.

"Ennui . . . er . . . Daphne . . . insinuated that if I knew a woman named Lila, I'd be much more likely to get the job. So, when Dr. Thorn assumed that this Lila person had recommended me for the job, I didn't correct him."

"Who is Lila?"

"I don't know." She hung her head, set down her fork. "I got the job over a dozen other applicants because I wasn't honest."

"It sounds like Enn—Daphne set you up to lie." Kade stroked his chin with his thumb. His thoughts shifted, rearranged. Maybe it was Daphne behind the thefts and not Thorn.

"I didn't want to do it." Allie wrung her hands. "I knew it was wrong, but I really needed this job. I can't move back in with my parents. Not when I'm finally carving out a life of my own." She pressed the heel of her palm to her forehead. "Wow, that sounds like an excuse."

"Don't be so hard on yourself." He rested a hand on her arm and she turned her palm up. She did it so automatically, as if it was the most natural thing in the world to turn to him for comfort, that a whiplash of fear cracked through him as startling and as potent as an explosion, blowing up across his nerve endings, blinding him with hot reality.

He was lying to her far worse than she was lying to Thorn. Holding back the truth to catch a thief, but at what cost to their relationship?

Kade had told so many lies as an undercover officer. Told himself it was necessary. Thought about how he'd lied to gain Angi's trust in order to infiltrate the drug gang.

For a split second, he was back at that apartment complex, his mouth hanging open in shocked disbelief as he stared at the young stripper's twisted neck and broken body—knowing he was in part responsible, that his lies had been an instrument of her death. His heart belted his chest, knocking against his ribs with hard, insistent raps.

"So, what should I do?" Allie whispered and raised her head, met his gaze with those magnificent purple-blue eyes. "Should I just go ahead and tell Dr. Thorn the truth? That I have no idea who Lila is, and let the chips fall where they may?"

Christ, he felt like a shitheel. Kade threaded his hands through his hair, then gently eased her upright in her chair. "No," he said, hating himself for it. "You need the job. It'll be over in a few weeks. If Thorn offers you a permanent position, you can tell him then."

"Yes." Allie nodded. "You're right. Don't rock the boat. That makes the most sense."

He smiled at her, feeling like a total fraud.

"Thanks," she said, glanced at the kitchen clock on the wall. "Oh my, is that the time? I've got to go." She pushed back her chair and so did he. "Last night was . . ." She blushed. "You were . . . well, maybe we can do this again sometime."

He had an overwhelming urge to tell her that all he wanted to do was stay in bed with her, that he wanted to get to know her better, that he cared about her, that he was falling in love with her.

But he couldn't do that.

And when she found out he'd been untruthful, and she didn't even know the real name of the man she'd slept with? Kade had an ugly feeling that his straight-arrow Rosy would kick his lying ass to the curb.

She looked at him with hope in those gorgeous eyes and he had no idea what to tell her, so he met her smile and mumbled, "Maybe."

Chapter Nine

MAYBE? ALLIE TEXTED Tasha as she left Rick's apartment. What the hell does that mean?

Tasha: Wait, what? U slept with him?

Allie: Don't judge. U went back to the guy who dumped U.

Tasha: Not judging. UR just not the type to sleep with a guy U have only known 10 days.

True enough, but Allie was changing. Shifting from the go-with-the-flow good girl into a woman who took charge of her sexuality and her life. She liked it, this change. Except for the "maybe" thing. What did that mean? Where did she stand with Rick?

Later, Allie texted as she reached the elevator, pocketed her phone, and stepped inside.

"Allie, hold the elevator!" a woman called.

She put her hand against the door to hold it open for the woman to catch up. It was Mindy Renfro, the manager of the Goodnight.

Mindy was fortyish, attractive, and recently divorced. She stepped breathless into the lift. "Thanks."

"Morning," Allie said.

"Good morning to you too." Mindy smiled like a fox in the henhouse. "Did I just see you coming out of Kade's apartment wearing the same clothes you had on yesterday?"

"Kade?" Allie frowned, perplexed. Did Rick's twin brother live in the same apartment? If so, why hadn't Rick mentioned it? "No, I was with Kade's twin brother, Rick."

Mindy looked as confused as Allie felt. "Huh? Kade doesn't have a twin."

"Yes, he does," Allie said, feeling a slippery, ugly sensation wriggle around in her belly.

Mindy shook her head. "I've known Kade Richmond since he was a kid. His mom and I are good friends."

Allie blinked, confused. If Kade Richmond lived in the apartment she just left, then who in the hell was Rick Braedon? Bigger question, who had she just had sex with?

Mindy's eyes grew wide and she slapped a palm over her mouth as if she'd just had an epiphany. "Oh, shit." She flapped her hands. "Never mind what I said. You're right. You spent the night with Rick. Forget everything else."

Stunned, Allie's brain struggled to keep up with the deluge of information. The picture on the wall of the cowboy bull rider had looked exactly like Rick. Was Kade actually Rick? If so, why would he lie about his identity?

Why? Well, you trusting little dumbass, he wanted to get you into bed, but that's all he wanted, so he lied about his name.

There was still something wrong with that assumption, but Allie couldn't quite put her finger on what it was. Mindy was acting super weird. She bolted from the elevator the minute the lift settled on the ground floor.

"Have a good day," Mindy called over her shoulder, and disappeared around the corner, leaving Allie dazed and perplexed.

Blistering shame crawled up Allie's spine, and she couldn't get past the truth. Rick, Kade, whatever his name might be, had intentionally duped her. Lied to her. Even though she couldn't figure out why, it was fact. What a gullible fool she was!

That's what you get for having sex with someone you barely know.

Shattered to her core, Allie stumbled to the second elevator that went to her wing of the apartment complex. All the happy afterglow she'd felt this morning dissolved into a puddle of pain.

Lies.

It all came back to lies.

Lies hurt.

Rick . . . Kade . . . had lied to her. She'd lied to Dr. Thorn. She thought about what Rick—crap, she kept forgetting that wasn't his name—what Kade had told her. He advised her against telling Dr. Thorn that she didn't know Lila. But, of course, that would be his advice. He was a liar.

Liars lied.

And she'd been lied to. Knew how badly it hurt. She couldn't keep lying to Dr. Thorn. If he fired her, so be it. If she had to move back home, so be it. Going home a failure was more honorable than lying.

Maybe Dr. Thorn would forgive her. Maybe not. Either way, she had to clear her conscience.

It might be a Pollyanna maneuver, a real rose-colored-glasses hope, but she chose honesty over deception. The truth had always worked for her. She had to trust it would work for her now.

AT EIGHT-THIRTY A.M. on Saturday morning, July 1, it was already ninety-seven degrees and expect to climb into the double digits by noon. Allie walked into the relief of the air conditioning in the main room of the popup art gallery where Daphne, aka Ennui, had led her on the day she was hired. The museum didn't open to the public until ten, but the Remington was already up, having arrived a half hour earlier.

Allie was thirty minutes late to work; it had taken her that long to stop trembling with hurt and fury at Kade. Anxiety twisted her up. She was on a mission to come clean, and she was pretty sure she was going to be fired.

And as far as Rick/Kade went? Well, she couldn't think about him right now.

Because underneath her anxiety lurked a swell of sad so big she could barely swallow. Would she be able to find her voice when she spoke to Dr. Thorn?

No one was in the exhibit room, which seemed unusual with the Remington freshly installed, but she knew the paintings were protected with twenty-four-hour security cameras, motion detectors, and Art Guard—playing-card-sized devices fixed to the backs of art canvases that emitted high-pitched screeching if the painting was unhooked from the wall mounts.

Heavy blackout curtains over the windows kept out the morning sun. The only lights in the room were the ones fixed underneath the paintings, casting the chamber in numerous shadows.

Hands clasped behind her back, she stepped up to the Remington for a better look. The artist in her was eager to assess the beauty of the brushstrokes, the woman in her desperate to get Kade off her mind. She studied the Remington a moment, cocked her head, bewildered by what she saw.

The door leading into Dr. Thorn's office opened and

he walked into the room. "Good morning, Allie," he greeted.

"Dr. Thorn," she said, turning in his direction, still puzzled by what she'd seen in the Remington. "I need to speak to you."

"Can it wait?" he asked, hurrying toward her. "I'm rushed for time. A VIP client is coming in to buy a piece of art."

"No," she said. "It can't wait, but this won't take long." *Because you'll be firing me as soon as you know the truth.*

He stopped, looked irritated. "What is it?"

Allie ironed her shoulders straight, tucked her chin in, pulled up her spine, making herself as tall as she could, ready to accept her licks. "I have to tell you something important."

He chuffed out a breath, folded his hands across his chest, scowled. "Well?"

Allie's heart knocked. He'd never been impatient or upset with her before. The good girl inside her wanted to mumble, "Never mind," and slink away, but she had to set things straight. "I lied," she said.

Dr. Thorn's expression didn't change. "About what?"

"Lila didn't recommend me for this job. I don't know anyone named Lila. Daphne suggested that if I pretended I knew Lila, I would get the job. I let you believe I knew this person, but I realize now that it was a mistake. It was wrong to let the lie persist, and I'm sorry."

"I know." Dr. Thorn shrugged as if she'd just told him she'd eaten the last donut and he was gluten free.

Huh? "How did you know?"

A tinge of a smile brushed his full lips. "Because there is no Lila."

"Wait." Allie pressed her second and third fingertips to her forehead. This had been a very mystifying morning, and she was beginning to think maybe she was trapped in some weird dream. "What?"

"It was a test," he said.

She thumped her forehead with her palm as if it might help process the information faster. "A test?"

"We needed to hire someone who was . . ." Dr. Thorn paused as if gauging his words carefully. "Suggestable."

Rankled, Allie frowned. "What does that mean?"

"You tend to go with the flow. You don't buck the status quo. That's what we needed. A follower who didn't have the guts to speak up."

Ouch! Her bottom lip trembled and a tiny muscle at the corner of her right eye jumped the way it did when her feelings got hurt. "Why do you think that about me?"

"You didn't deny knowing Lila. You went with the flow."

Well, she had denied it at first, but her desire to land the job had won out. "And going with the flow is a bad thing?"

"No," he said. "That's precisely why we hired you. Because you don't ask questions. You trust others to know what's best for you."

He was calling her gullible? Allie was insulted, even as she acknowledged the truth of her naivety. She *did* trust too easily, assumed other people's motives were as pure as her own.

Why? Why was she so trusting? Stupid! Kade's betrayal had taught her the fallacy of trusting the wrong people.

A kernel of anger knotted up inside her stomach, took root, grew, popped. She was tired of being made a patsy.

"Actually, Dr. Thorn, that's not true," she said sharply. "Because I have questions, lots of questions. One important question, in particular."

"What's that?" he asked, looking a little less certain of her than before.

Bolstered, indignant, she sank her hands on her hips. "Why is there a fake Remington hanging in place of the real one?"

He laughed, flinty and fast. "You noticed."

"Of course I noticed. I have a master's degree in fine art. Do you think I'm an idiot?"

He shrugged, a blasé lift of his shoulders, as if to say, *Yeah, I did.* That pissed her off even more. "Listen, it's no big deal. The museum curator was uneasy about putting the real Remington in the popup with the rolling blackouts going on, so he put up a duplicate instead."

"That's cheating the museumgoers," she said, feeling the anger building hotter inside of her.

"The *Mona Lisa* is behind bulletproof Plexiglas. Does that cheat the museumgoers?"

"Yes, actually it does. But it is the *Mona Lisa* and it's been stolen before. She *is* the most famous painting in the world and requires protection."

"And the Remington doesn't just because it's not as highly valued?" His upper lip curled into a snarl.

Something was fishy here. If they were that worried about the Remington, why not leave it out of the event entirely instead of putting up a fake? "Where is the real Remington?"

"In a safe place."

Allie didn't believe that, not for a second. She was done blindly trusting people and taking them at their word. "I want to see it."

His face was unmovable, stony as a gargoyle. "And if I say no?"

"I'm going to call the museum curator at the Sid Richardson," she said, "and get to the bottom of this." Blood pounding crazy fast through her temples, Allie turned on her heels, headed for the exit.

That was when Thorn lunged for her.

"Kade," Mindy Renfro called to him as he headed through the lobby of the Goodnight. "I think I might have blown your cover."

He froze, pivoted, came back to where Mindy was sticking her head out of her office. "What do you mean?"

"I saw Allie Grainger coming out of your apartment—

by the way, good choice, she's an awesome girl—and I dropped your name. I didn't know you were going by an alias with her. I'm truly sorry."

"What did she say?" he asked, resisting the urge to curse. He couldn't begin to imagine what Allie must be thinking about him right now.

"She didn't say much, but she looked pretty upset. I hope you can smooth things over with her. You two would be so good together."

Crap. He hadn't even thought about Mindy knowing the both of them when he'd brought Allie back to his apartment. Hell, he hadn't thought about much of anything except getting her into his bed. He was going to have to do some serious groveling to mend this.

"Thanks for letting me know, Mindy," he said. He couldn't blame the apartment manager. He was the fool for mixing business with pleasure.

Shoving a hand through his hair, he hurried to the parking lot for his pickup. His phone dinged, letting him know he had a text.

After Allie had left his apartment, he'd texted his point person at the FBI to ask if there had been any power outages during the popup art galleries in the other cities where the paintings had gone missing.

Confirmed, texted the FBI agent. Power outages during all eleven popups where paintings were stolen.

Kade texted: That must be when Thorn switched the paintings with the forgeries.

FBI agent: Most likely.

Kade: Check with the power company to see if it was really rolling blackouts or if someone hacked the power gird.

FBI agent: On it.

Kade pocketed his phone and strode toward his truck, his mind turning over everything that had happened that morning. His job might be to catch Thorn before he stole the Remington, but his mission was to find Allie and set things straight. It killed him to think that he'd hurt her.

The streets were quiet when he arrived at the courthouse. The Twilight town square thrived on the tourist trade, and most buildings were closed to until ten. He didn't expect the main entrance to be open, but he knew Allie entered through the rear door when she went in early.

He drove into the side lot, spied Thorn's car parked beside Allie's. His gut kicked and the hairs on his arms lifted, and he just *knew*, as if by some strange telepathy, that Allie was in trouble.

Gun. Glove compartment. Now.

He didn't question his instincts. Grabbed his duty weapon and slipped in through the back door and into the popup museum just in time to see Thorn tackle Allie to the ground.

She shrieked, and her terrified sound sent ice through his bones.

"Twilight Police Department," Kade growled, gun in one hand, badge in the other. "Let the girl go!"

Chapter Ten

HUH? TWILIGHT POLICE DEPARTMENT?

The words barely sank into her fear-paralyzed brain.

Kade was a police officer? A blip of joy exploded inside her heart because if he was law enforcement that meant he had a very good reason for lying to her, but she had no time to process this new information.

Instead of letting her go, Thorn got her in a choke-hold, dragged her to her feet, and used her body as a shield between him and Kade. She could barely breathe, much less form a coherent thought.

Thorn tightened his grip.

Her vision dimmed, blurred. In front of her, she could barely make out Kade's tall form. He was holler-ing something, but all she heard was a loud whoosh-ing noise, as if she were traveling through a long, dark tunnel.

She kicked at him feebly, strained hard to hear what Kade was saying.

"Let her go, Thorn," Kade yelled. "Don't cross that line. Right now, the only thing you're in trouble for is art theft. You hurt her, and you're looking at serious prison time."

"You don't get it," Thorn snarled. "All my life, I've struggled for recognition from the artistic elite. They called *my* art 'pedestrian' and 'derivative.'"

"You stole the paintings to prove you're a great artist?" Kade asked.

"I showed those bastards," Thorn crowed. "I stole their so-called 'works of art' and replaced them with my forgeries and no one noticed! I'm as good as those artists ever were. Better even!"

"I noticed," Allie rasped around the pressure of Thorn's elbow at her throat.

The crook of Thorn's elbow was a noose, choking her. Allie couldn't breathe, and her lungs were aching.

"You hurt her, you son-of-a-bitch, and I'll kill you with my bare hands." Kade's voice was a solid wall of rage.

"Put the gun down," Thorn said, squeezing Allie's neck with more pressure than she could stand.

Her eyes popped. Head throbbed. Her tongue seemed to swell, blocking off her airway. Terror had a name, and it was Dr. Thorn.

Trust, whispered the voice that always guided her to safety.

No. She'd spent too many years depending on someone else to save her.

Trust in yourself, the voice in her head corrected. *You save you.*

What a time to learn a lesson. Yes, she had to stop trusting that if she gave up control, she would be okay. It had worked for her as a child on a cancer ward, and later in life it had worked because her parents had always been there to catch her when she fell. But she was twenty-four years old now and healthy as a horse. It was time to step up to the plate and save herself.

That didn't mean she had to stop trusting people, become jaded and cynical. Rather, it was time for discernment. Figure out when it was okay to trust and go with the flow and when she needed to put up her dukes and fight.

This was the time for fighting.

Allie summoned every ounce of strength she had in her, which, granted, considering she was light-headed from lack of oxygen, wasn't much. As hard as she could, Allie jammed her elbow backward, aiming for Thorn's solar plexus.

"Oof!" Thorn grunted and leaned away from her, but he did not let go. The momentum of the impact tipped him backward. He fell, taking her with him.

Allie heard running footsteps as Kade raced toward them.

And then the lights went out.

THE CAVERNOUS ROOM was pitch black.

Kade couldn't react fast enough to the sudden extinguishing of the light and he tripped over someone in the dark.

"Allie!" he cried.

It must have been Thorn, because a hand closed around his ankle and Kade went down. His gun flew from his hand, spun across the floor. He heard his service revolver clink against something and he tried to gauge how far away it might be, but Thorn was on him, straddling his body, punching him in the face.

Fine. As long as Thorn was punching him, that meant he no longer had hold of Allie.

Kade scrabbled, clawing for Thorn's wrists, missed. Got another fist to the face. He grunted against the pain, tasted blood. Damn it all. Fast as he could, he wrapped his legs around Thorn's waist, and they were in a free-for-all tussle.

Clenching his jaw, he smacked his forehead into Thorn's, heard the loud crack, felt the impact jolt through his neck, slam down his spine.

He must have busted Thorn's nose, because a shower of blood spattered across his face. Thorn punched him again, and Kade's bottom lip split open.

Kade kicked Thorn off him, wriggled on his back across the floor, hands out, searching for his gun. Thorn grabbed Kade by his feet, yelled like a conquering ape, and hauled him back. For a stout man, he was surprisingly adroit.

Thorn was on his feet, kicking Kade so hard that all he could do was roll into a ball and cover his head with his arms to protect himself. He was down and out, and it was too dark to see the kicks coming.

But he felt them. Each and every one.

When he tried to flip onto his back, the tip of Thorn's shoe caught him in the gut, knocking the air from his body. Kade gasped, wheezed, drooled. It felt like hours had passed, but it had probably no more than a couple of minutes since the lights went out.

Snap out of it. Get the upper hand.

Yeah, not so easy to do when sledgehammers were pounding inside his head and he couldn't see a damn thing. But even in his blind pain, Kade was thinking of Allie. Where was she? Had she gotten away?

Then a truly horrifying thought occurred to him. Thorn had been choking her hard. What if she was unconscious?

Or worse . . .

No, no, she couldn't be dead. Not before he had a chance to apologize. Not before they had a chance to know each other. Not before he could tell her he was falling in love with her.

He was still gasping for air, Thorn still kicking, in a mad rage now. Kade heard his ribs crack, and he screamed against the sharp pain, doubled over. If he didn't do something soon, he was going to black out.

Thorn went for the kill. A tornado of kicks. The more Kade tried to move, the harder he kicked.

Stay down, said his instinct.

Get up, yelled his manhood.

Suddenly, the room was bathed in bright morning light. Temporarily stunned, he and Thorn both froze in the middle of their crazy tableau and squinted at the shocking sunlight streaming through the window where Allie had crawled over to rip down the thick, heavy curtain.

She stood there, chest heaving, Kade's duty weapon clutched in both her hands, hair wild, eyes wide, looking like the fiercest warrior woman he'd ever seen.

"Step away from him, Thorn," she growled like a puma, "or I'll shoot your dick off."

And damn if Kade didn't laugh through the pain.

THE MINUTES IMMEDIATELY following Allie's showdown with Thorn went all Monet—fuzzy, indistinct, but incredibly powerful.

She stood trying to figure out what to do next, gun trained on her boss, her hands shaking, her heart in shreds at the sight of Kade's battered, bleeding body, trying to wrap her head around what was going on.

Before she could make sense of it all, the front door slammed open and a team of federal officers poured into the room. Guns drawn. "FBI! Put the weapon down! Now!"

One of the men was dragging a sulky Ennui/Daphne into the room behind him.

Allie put the gun on the ground, raised her hands over her head, feeling both badass and bushwhacked. Every cell in her body tingled, fully alive.

It took the FBI a bit to sort out who was who. They arrested Thorn and Ennui and the ambulance arrived to take Kade away.

"Is he going to be okay?" Allie asked, hugging herself.

"He took a licking," said one of the FBI agents. "But he'll keep on ticking."

"Can I talk to him?"

"Not now," the agent said.

"When?" She knitted her fingers together.

"I need to take your statement first. You can go see him at the hospital after."

"He saved my life," Allie whispered.

"Lady," said the agent, "from where I'm standing, you saved his. If you hadn't gotten the upper hand when you did, who knows what would have happened? Now, have a seat, and let the paramedics check you out too before we get to the interview."

It took precisely an hour, and by the time they'd finished, Allie had gleaned a few details about the case. She learned Thorn had been under FBI investigation for months, and hacker Daphne, who turned out to be his niece, had been helping him by shutting down the electrical grids and causing the rolling blackouts, during which time, Thorn would switch out his forgeries for the works of art. Thorn was motivated by his ego and the narcissistic belief that he was a better painter than the masters. He took joy in knowing his paintings hung in galleries in place of the originals and that no one had been the wiser.

That didn't make much sense to Allie. No one but Thorn and Ennui knew they were his paintings hanging in the galleries until the last theft, and the forged George Rodrigue in New Orleans had prompted the Feds to dig into the popup art galleries around the country and they discovered the other forgeries.

Daphne, on the other hand, had been in it purely for the money. Thorn gave her the real works of art, which she in turn sold on the deep web.

Allie notified her boss at the Visitors Center that she was taking the day off and headed for the hospital. But by the time she got there, Kade had already been treated and released. That was a relief. If he'd been seriously injured, they would have admitted him.

Feeling nervous, she went home, only to find reporters hanging around her apartment complex. She ducked her head and pushed past them as they threw questions at her. How had they gotten here so fast?

"*You were working for Dr. Thorn. Did you have any idea he was a thief?*"

"*Do you know where the real Remington is?*"

"*Weren't you the one who spotted the fake?*"

"*What's your relationship to Detective Kade Richmond?*"

Mindy held the door open. "Pack of jackals," she hollered at the reporters. To Allie she said, "Get in here, kid."

"Wow, that's intimidating," Allie said.

"No worries." Mindy waved a hand. "They'll be off when more interesting news breaks."

"I hope that's soon."

"You're a hero." Mindy laughed. "Enjoy fame while it's happening. How's Kade?"

"I don't know." Allie fidgeted, shifting her weight from foot to foot. "He got beat up pretty badly. I tried to see him at the hospital, but he was already gone."

"Probably went to recuperate at his mom's."

Speaking of moms, Allie's cell phone was pinging with texts from her mother. "I better go call my mom. Let her know I'm okay."

"Sure, sure." Mindy waved her away.

Allie let herself into her apartment, dropped her purse down on the floor, and rested her back against the door, her legs still left loose and unreliable from the spent adrenaline. She slid down until her butt hit the cool tile floor, drew her legs to her chest, rested her head on her knees, and let the cleansing tears flow.

A loud knock sounded against the door. Allie startled, jumped to her feet, swiped at her face. Probably some sneaky reporter who'd gotten past Mindy. She put her eye to the peephole.

There stood Ric—Kade. His western shirt was unbuttoned, revealing a chest swathed in bandages, supporting broken ribs. His face was battered, bruised and cut. His right eye was swollen partially shut.

Allie winced and opened the door.

"Hey," he said, giving her a crooked smile that immediately turned into a grimace of pain.

Her heart did a crazy hop-skip and she tried not to let her joy at seeing him show. "Hi."

"Can I come in?" His eyes darkened, tone lowered.

Without saying a word, she stepped aside, motioned him into the sitting area, but he didn't sit. They stood staring at each other. She couldn't get a read on him.

"Have you been crying?"

"Yes," she said, done forever with lying.

"Over me?" He gulped so hard his Adam's apple bobbed.

Oh, the ego on this one. "Stress release," she said. "You might be used to violent confrontations, but I'm not."

"I'm sorry I dragged you into all this."

"How are you?" she asked, not addressing that comment.

"Not dead, thanks to you." His grin was shallow as he avoided smiling too wide.

"You saved me a couple of times." She shrugged like she didn't care. "It was my turn to save you."

"We make a good team."

Allie bit her bottom lip, determined not to let him charm her. It would be so easy to forgive him everything, but she wasn't so gullible anymore, not so easily swayed by a sexy grin and handsome face. She crossed her arms over her chest, waited to hear what he had to say.

"Listen," he said. "I'm sorry I lied to you about who I was."

"I get it. You're an undercover cop." She kept her voice steady.

"I wanted to tell you—"

"But I was a suspect."

He nodded, looked contrite.

"That's why you started hanging out with me?" She pressed her tongue to the roof of her mouth to stave off emotions she didn't want to feel.

"It was," he said, his honesty a battering ram, knocking her hard in the gut. "But I was attracted to you right from the start."

"You used me to get information on Thorn."

"I'm sorry. Please forgive me. Allie, I wanted . . . What happened between us wasn't supposed to happen, but it did. I have feelings for you."

"I have . . . *had* . . . feelings for you too but I can't trust those feelings because they were based on a lie."

His nod was slower, sadder this time. "I get it."

"I don't even know who you are."

His eyes glinted in the light, and his bloodied, puffy bottom lip trembled oh so slightly. Or maybe it was just her imagination. "I'd like to start over. Get to know you properly. Go on a real date—"

"Ri—Kade, I can't. I can't even remember your real name."

"You could forgive me," he said.

"I'm sorry. I just can't trust my feelings anymore. It's like you told me. I have to stop trusting so easily, be more discerning."

His laugh was rugged and rueful. "When I said that, I never thought it would come back to bite me in the ass."

"I never thought I'd be in a position to take that advice, but because of you, I am."

"There's nothing I can do to make this right?" he murmured.

"Goodbye, Kade," she said, wanting him out of the apartment before she burst into tears again. She moved to the front door, held it open.

Without another word, he plunked his Stetson down on his head and walked away.

Chapter Eleven

KADE HAD NO more strolled out the door than Allie's mother called. She answered, "Hi, Mom."

"Oh, sweetie, I saw you on the news. Are you okay?"

"Fine, fine." She lifted a hand to her bruised neck. No need to bring that up now.

"They're saying you're a hero. Saving a cop who was being assaulted by an art thief. My goodness, I didn't know your profession was so dangerous."

Allie grinned. Ah, so this was where she got her naivety. "It's not, Mom. This was a fluke occurrence."

"But art thieves are a real threat."

"Not really. I can take care of myself."

"Yes, but maybe you should go back to school, get a safer career."

It dawned on her that the reason her mother was so overprotective wasn't because she feared Allie couldn't take care of herself, but that she would no longer have a purpose if her daughter didn't need her.

"I'll always need you, Mom," she said gently. "Just not for every little thing."

"You call tussling with a criminal *little*?"

"I did what I had to do, and I came out ahead."

Her mother sighed softly. "You really are all grown up, aren't you?"

"Yes, but that's how it should be. Remember when I was first diagnosed with cancer and you were scared you'd never get to see me grow up?"

"Those were horrible days."

"We got through them."

"Your belief in healing made your cancer disappear."

"I wouldn't say that. I just got lucky that I was the one in a hundred thousand that had a spontaneous remission."

"We got a miracle, and I still couldn't trust it . . . but you did. Here I was, thinking I was protecting you from the world, when all along you were instinctively taking care of yourself." Her mother's voice held an incredulous note, as if she'd just had a big epiphany. "I don't have to worry about you anymore."

"You're my mom, you'll always worry."

Her mother laughed, a sound of joy and relief. "That's true, but I can stop smothering you."

"I know you were always coming from a place of love."

"My bright little daughter," she whispered. "My shining star."

"Love you, Mom."

"Love you too, sweetheart. Can you come to Sunday dinner now that the whole popup museum thing is kaput?"

"Absolutely."

"See you then, darling."

Allie switched off her phone, and for the first time in her life, felt free. This whole experience, taxing as it might have been, had changed her for life. She was a brand-new person, and she could handle anything and still keep her heart open.

In the span of a week, Kade had taught her so many life lessons, and she was grateful for that, but she still didn't know if she could find her way back to trusting him.

But she wanted to try.

"Damn fine police work, Richmond," Kade's boss, Captain Finn, told him a week after Thorn's arrest.

One week, seven long days, without seeing or hearing from Allie. It was killing Kade to stay away from her, but she'd made it clear that she didn't trust her feelings because of his lie, and he had to respect her wishes.

"The Feds are happy, I'm happy. You're getting kicked upstairs if you still want the promotion."

Except Kade wasn't happy. Yes, he wanted the promotion, but in the pursuit of it, he'd lost Allie.

Finn eyed him speculatively. "You sure you want to leave vice? You're our best undercover detective."

"Yeah," Kade said, thinking of Allie. "And that's the problem. Undercover changes you. I've lost myself in the deception. It's time to reclaim my identity."

Finn nodded, understanding. "That thing with the stripper really got to you."

"Angi," Kade murmured. "Her name was Angi."

"You weren't responsible for her death."

"Logically, I know that . . . but in here . . ." He tapped his heart with a fist. "I'm guilty. I need a fresh start."

"I get it." Captain Finn thrust out his palm. "We're going to miss your ugly mug."

Kade shook his hand. "I'll drop by now and again, just to annoy you."

"I'm counting on it." Finn grinned. "Now get the hell out of my office."

Kade walked out of the police station feeling lighter, freer, released from the prison that his undercover assignment had become. Thorn was going to pay for his crimes, Kade had gotten his promotion, and the only thing missing was Allie.

He'd blown it. So what if he was so crazy about her that he couldn't think straight? She didn't trust him, and without trust, how could they ever have a functional relationship?

Head down, he took the steps two at a time, headed for the curb where he'd parallel parked. He reached the last step, glanced up, and that was when he saw her standing by his truck.

His Allie.

Their eyes met. She smiled that unicorn smile of hers. His heart softened, melted at the explosion of rainbows.

What was she doing here?

THAT SMILE WAS all Allie needed to see to know she'd made the right choice in hanging around the police station to wait for him after she'd completed a follow-up interview.

Kade sauntered toward her, his grin growing bigger the closer he got, genuine happiness on that endearing face that was still healing from Thorn's beating. Kade stopped a few feet away as if wanting to make sure she wasn't pulling some kind of "gotcha" trick on him before coming closer.

"Hi," he said, his eyes searching hers.

"Hey."

"Why are you here?" he asked.

She waved a hand in the direction of the building. "Follow-up on the Thorn thing. They're dotting their Is and crossing their Ts. He's going down."

"Oh," he said, the light dimming in his eyes.

"But that interview was over half an hour ago. I stayed because I wanted to see you."

His helpless smile was back, joyful, infectious, and Allie returned it with an I'm-all-in grin.

"I haven't seen you around the apartment complex," he said.

"I've been staying with my parents in Fort Worth."

"To avoid me?"

"Partially," she admitted. "I needed some time to think things through."

"Are you moving back in with them permanently?"

"No."

"Did you find another job?" he asked.

She shook her head, enjoying the suspense of keeping him on tenterhooks. "No."

"Found another roommate?" He came closer until they were standing toe-to-toe.

She peered up at him, feeling the hot sun on her skin, loving it. Loving this moment. "That depends."

"On what?"

"If he's available to move in with me."

Kade's eyes widened and his mouth thinned. "You're moving in with another guy?"

"No," she laughed. "Silly man, I'm asking *you* to be my roommate."

"You mean . . ." His voice caught. "You want me to move in with you?"

She nodded, suddenly unable to find her voice.

"I can't believe you're actually suggesting we live together. I'm floored, I thought you didn't trust me."

Allie giggled, an effervescent giddiness rising like bubbles into her throat. "My feelings were hurt," she admitted. "I tried not to trust you, but my inner voice told me you were The One."

"Your inner voice," he murmured, wrapping his arms around her waist and drawing her closer to him. "The one that never steers you wrong?"

"That'd be the one," she whispered.

"I'll need a little time to think about it," he drawled.

"How little?" she teased. She could tell from the way he was holding her and looking at her that he was joking.

"With you," he said, "no time at all."

"There're a few things we need to iron out first. Leaving underwear on the bathroom floor could be a deal breaker."

"Aww," he said. "I was looking forward to stripping off your skimpy panties and throwing them on the bathroom floor."

"Okay," she amended. "One-hour rule. Underwear can stay on the floor for up to an hour in the case of panty stripping."

"One hour?" he said. "What if our playtime goes longer?"

She giggled, melded against him. "All right, two hours."

"Honey, the time that we were together, we were at it for hours and hours."

"Oh, hell," she said. "Leave our underwear wherever you want."

"Going along to get along?" he asked.

"No," she said. "I'm just anxious to get you back in bed."

"Well, why didn't you say so, sweetheart? I can make that happen right now." He cupped her chin between his palms, tipped her face up to meet his, his dark eyes peering into her as if he were jumping into a bottomless well and happy for the fall. "This is going to be magical."

"How can you be so sure? There are lots of ups and downs living with someone else."

"Because it's *you*, Allie Grainger. Sure, there are lots of bumps in the road, but *you're* what makes it worth the ride."

"So says the rodeo cowboy."

"And that means I ought to know."

"Ride 'em, cowboy."

He ducked his head, his mouth inches from hers. His hands on her cheeks. "That's exactly what I intend on doing."

With that, he kissed her, and all doubts vanished in the heat of his sizzling-hot kiss.

The following is a sneak
peek at Lori Wilde's newest
Twilight, Texas, Christmas novel

THE CHRISTMAS DARE

On sale October 2019
wherever your favorite books are sold!

A jilted-at-the-altar bride reunites with her high
school sweetheart in Lori Wilde's sensational
new Twilight, Texas, Christmas novel!

Kelsey James always played by the rules and look where
it got her—dumped and half-drunk in a poofy white
dress, her Christmas wedding ruined. Then her best
friend talks her into going on her "honeymoon" anyway,
daring her to a "Christmas of Yes." It's about time she
lets loose a little, so Kelsey agrees to say yes to fun, to
romance, and to adventure! And adventure leads her
right smack into the arms of sexy Noah MacGregor.

Noah's never one to say no to a risk—from leading his
NBA team to victory to making Christmas cookies in
Twilight, he's up to the challenge! But a lot has gone on
since they were teenagers, and he knows he has to take his
time to make Kelsey dare to believe that what they feel
is more than just the holiday magic that's in the air . . .

Chapter One

ON A CHRISTMAS-SCENTED Saturday morning in early December, Dallas's newly elected mayor, Filomena James, walked her only surviving daughter, Kelsey, down the pew-packed aisle of the lavishly decorated Highland Park United Methodist Church.

She slipped her arm through her daughter's, and off they went to the instrumental score of "Let Me Tell You About My Boat." Filomena had insisted on music hipper than "The Wedding March" for her child's big day.

Bucking the old guard.

That was how she won her mayoral seat. Filomena was innovative, clever, and resourceful. Never mind that Kelsey was a traditionalist. After all, Filomena was the one shelling out the big bucks for this shindig, and to quote her campaign buttons, *she* was the "rebel with a cause."

She'd insisted on the December wedding date, so as not to conflict with her mayoral bid. In mild protest, Kelsey put up a feeble fuss. Her daughter was not a fan of December in general or Christmas in particular. But as always, Filomena had prevailed.

"Lucky" for Kelsey, Mama knew best.

Everything was going as Filomena had planned. That is until the groom hightailed it for the exit, elbows locked with his best man.

Fifteen minutes later, back in the bridal room of the church, Kelsey sat as calm as a statue, ankles crossed demurely, feet tucked underneath the bench, expression mild. Her waist-length hair twisted high in an elegant braided chignon. A bouquet of white roses and a crumpled, handwritten Dear Jane letter were lying in her lap.

Sounds of car doors slamming and hushed voices stirring gossip drifted in through the partially opened window.

The poor thing.

Do you think Kelsey suspected Clive was gay?

How does Filomena recover from this?

Exhaling deeply, Kelsey hid her smile as relief poured through her. Okay, sprinkle in a dab of sadness, a jigger of regret, and a dollop of I-do-not-want-to-face-my-mother, but other than that, Clive's abrupt adios hadn't peeled her back too far.

Hey, it wasn't the most embarrassing thing that had ever happened to her. She'd get through this.

Filomena paced. As if struck by a hundred flyswatters all slapping at once, her cheeks flushed scarlet. Black Joan Crawford eyebrows pulled into a hard V. "Do you have any idea how humiliated *I* am?" she howled.

"I'm sorry, Mother," Kelsey said by rote.

"This is your fault. If you'd slept with Clive, as I told you to, instead of sticking to that wait-until-the-wedding nonsense, *I* would not be on the hook for this nightmare."

"Yes, Mother. You're right. You're always right."

Filomena's scowl lessened. "Well, at least you admit it."

Kelsey's best friend, Tasha Williams, who'd been standing by the door, lifted the hem of her emerald green, charmeuse maid of honor dress and strode across the small room to toe off with the mayor-elect.

"Are you frigging kidding me?" Tasha's deep brown eyes narrowed and she planted her hands onto her hips, head bobbing as she spoke. "Kels got stood up, not *you*."

Yay, you. Grateful, Kelsey sent her friend a thank-you smile.

"The media will eat me for dinner over this." Through flinty eyes, Filomena's glower could wither houseplants to dust.

Uh-oh, Kelsey knew the look far too well. A clear signal to give her mother a Grand Canyon–sized berth.

"Have an inch of compassion, you witch." Tasha glared lasers at Filomena.

Proud that her bestie had not called her mother a "bitch" when she knew the word was searing the end of Tasha's tongue, Kelsey cleared her throat. Long ago, she'd learned not to throw emotional gasoline on her mother's fits of pique. Courting head-to-toe, third-degree burns was *not* her favorite pastime.

"What did you say to me?" A sharp, cutting tone curdled her mother's voice. Her icy stare could quell Katniss Everdeen.

Gulping, Tasha couldn't quite meet Filomena's eyes. "Just . . . just . . . have a heart, dammit. She's your daughter."

"Don't you lecture me, you little upstart." Filomena shoved her face in front of Tasha's nose.

In a soothing, even tone, Kelsey pressed her palms downward. "Mom, I'm fine here. Please, go do damage control. You'll find a way to turn this to your advantage. You're a master at spinning gold from straw."

"Excellent idea." With stiff-legged movements, Filomena shifted her attention off Tasha. Finger pinching the ruching at the waist of her snug-fitting mother-of-the-bride dress, she straightened herself, dusted off her shoulders, and stalked toward the door. "Clive's father owes me big-time."

Filomena's exit left Kelsey and Tasha exhaling simultaneously.

"Ah, gotta love how she turns every disaster into a political stepping stone," Tasha muttered.

"It's her superpower," Kelsey said.

"What's her kryptonite?"

Rereading Clive's scrawled letter, Kelsey didn't answer. Before Clive fled with Kevin, he'd pressed the note into the minister's hand.

Dear Kelsey,

Shabby of me to ditch you this way, but please believe me when I say I wanted to marry you. You are the kindest, most loving person I've ever met and my deep affection for you has gotten me this far. But no more cowering in the closet, praying to turn into something I'm not. You deserve better. I deserve better. I've been a coward, and you were safe. Time to stop running. Kevin and I love each other. We have for a long time. Last night after the bachelor party . . . well . . . let's just say everything changed forever. Out there somewhere is the real love of your life. Please, cash in the honeymoon tickets and spoil yourself with a trip of your own.

Best wishes,
Your friend always, Clive

Floating off the page, three words stood tall above the others, accusing her of her most glaring shortcoming.

You were safe.

Yes, she played it safe.

Without question.

Guilty as charged.

While Clive's betrayal stung, the loss and embarrassment didn't equal the pain of the truth. If she hadn't been playing it safe, going for the most accommodating, least challenging man around, she wouldn't have ended up here.

Once again, her mother was right, and this *was* her

fault. To avoid a major war that she stood no chance of winning, Kelsey had kept her own wants and needs suppressed. Filomena pushed the union because Clive's father was Texas Supreme Court Justice Owen Patterson. Kelsey had meekly accepted the union.

Intelligent, witty, urbane, Clive was entertaining and erudite, and he always smelled fantastic. How easily she'd slipped into a tranquil relationship with him. When he'd told her that he was old-fashioned and wanted to wait until the wedding night before they had sex, she'd been charmed.

And it was a major red flag she'd blown right past.

"'Sweet' is code for boring," Tasha had warned when Kelsey broke the news that she and Clive weren't having sex. "Who buys a car without test driving it first?"

Now she understood why Clive avoided having sex with her. Not because she was special as he'd claimed. Nope, because he wasn't really interested. She was gullible and had taken him at his word.

What a dumbass. Wadding the letter in her fist, Kelsey tossed it into the wicker wastebasket.

"Good start." Tasha gave a gleeful grin. "Let's cash in those tickets and get this party started. You need a wild night with a hot guy. How long has it been since you've had sex?"

Well over eighteen months. Since long before she'd started dating Clive. "I don't know if I'm ready for that."

"Will you stop? You gotta get back out there. Time's a-wastin'." Tasha reached for her clutch purse, popped it open, and took out a fifth of Fireball whiskey. "I brought this for the wedding reception, but we need it *ASAP*."

"Believe me." Kelsey held up a palm. "I'm mad at myself for letting things get this far. I should have stopped the wedding, but my mother started the steamroller, and I just climbed aboard the way I always do."

"Reason enough to take a shot." Tasha chugged a mouthful of hooch, let loose with a satisfied burp, and pressed the whiskey into Kelsey's hand.

"I don't—"

"Drink," Tasha commanded.

"Good gravy, I'm not wrecked. I promise."

"But you *should* get wrecked. Get mad. Howl at the moon. Let loose." Tasha stuck her arms out at her sides as if she was an airplane. "Wing woman at your service. Never fear, Tasha is here."

Sighing, Kelsey wondered if her friend had a point. Who would judge her for getting drunk after being jilted at the altar?

With a toss of her head, she took a short swallow. The cinnamon-flavored whiskey burned and lit a warm liquid fire in the pit of her stomach.

"Take another," Tasha coached.

Opening her mouth to say no, three words flashed vivid neon in Kelsey's mind. *You were safe.*

Clive nailed it. Since her twin sister, Chelsea, drowned on Possum Kingdom Lake when they were ten, she'd been playing it safe. Honestly, even before then. "Safe" was her factory default setting. Chelsea's death only compounded her natural peacemaking tendency. No adventuresome twin around to balance her out.

With a snort, Kelsey took another drink. Longer this time, and she felt her insides unspool.

"Good girl." Tasha patted Kelsey's shoulder.

After the third shot, Kelsey felt warm and woozy and ten times better than she had half an hour ago.

"Okay, okay." With a worried expression, Tasha took the bottle away from her. "All things in moderation. I don't want to hold your hair while you puke before we ever get out of the church."

Snapping her fingers, Kelsey reached for the bottle. "Gimme, I'm done playing by the rules."

Ninja quick, Tasha hid the whiskey behind her back. "I've created a monster. I'll return it when we're in the limo."

"Bye-bye limo." Kelsey hiccupped. "Clive and Kevin took it."

"How do you know?"

"Peek at the curb."

Poking her head out the window, Tasha said. "Oh well. Uber here we come."

"Where are we going?"

"Wherever you want. In place of a honeymoon, we'll spend the next two weeks doing something wild and crazy. *Fun, fun, fun* are our buzzwords."

"Don't you have a job?"

Spinning her finger in the air helicopter-blade style, Tasha said, "I quit last week."

"Wait. What? Why?"

"Had a fight with my boss. He pinched my ass and I slapped his face, yada, yada, he wins."

"Oh Tash, I'm so sorry. Did you consult a lawyer?"

"No need. Handled it on social media." Buffing her knuckles against her shirt, Tasha grinned. "Since he owns his own business, he can't get fired, but you can bet he got a lot of angry comments and people saying they won't be using his catering company."

"Why didn't I know about this?" Kelsey asked as guilt gnawed. She'd been a shitty friend. "Why didn't you tell me?"

"Wedding prep and getting your mother elected mayor of Dallas kept you snowed. When did you have time for my drama?"

"What are friends for? I need to make it up to you."

"Then kick up your heels."

"Shouldn't you be scouting another job instead of holding my hand?"

"No worries. Already got a new one."

"When? Where?"

"You're looking at the new executive chef for La Fonda's, and I start the Monday after the New Year."

"That's awesome! I mean about the executive chef job, not getting your ass pinched. Congrats."

"Let's do this thing." With one palm raised in the air as if she was a waiter balancing a tray, Tasha pumped her hand. "Celebrate my new job and your freedom at the same time. We'll have an epic adventure."

"No doubt." She mulled over Tasha's proposition. Why not? Time to break out of her bubble.

"Where should we go? New Orleans? Eat gumbo, drink hurricanes, and get inked?" Tasha wriggled her eyebrows. "What do you think about me getting a spider tattoo on my neck?"

Wincing, Kelsey sucked in a breath through clenched teeth. "Hmm, Cajun food upsets my stomach."

"Vegas? Blow through our mad money, pick up male strippers?"

"Um, I want something more—"

"Kelsey-ish?"

Sedate was the word that had popped into her head. Sedate. Sedative. She'd been comatose too long. "Where would *you* prefer to go, Tasha? Whatever you decide, I'm good with it.

Tasha gave an exaggerated eye roll. "Girl, you got dumped on your wedding day, and I can find a party wherever I go, even in your white bread world."

She adored Tasha's spunkiness. Spunk was also the reason Filomena wasn't a big Tasha fan.

Five years earlier, Tasha and Kelsey had met when Kelsey was organizing a fundraiser during her mother's bid for a city council seat. In charge of hiring the caterers for the event at the Dallas Museum of Art, Kelsey had gone to interview Tasha's boss, Tony, the ass pincher, without knowing of course that he was the kind of person who sexually harassed his employees.

When Tasha popped a mini quiche into Kelsey's

mouth, and it was the best damn thing she'd ever eaten, she'd hired the caterer on the spot, based solely on Tasha's cooking skills. After hitting it off, Kelsey stuck around to help Tasha clean up after the gala, and the rest belonged in the annals of BFF history.

"Wherever we go there must be scads of hot *straight* guys," Tasha said. "How does a dude ranch sound?"

"Good heavens, I have no idea how to ride a horse."

"Yeah, me neither."

"Wherever you want, I'll go."

"Don't make me pick. I always pick, this is for *you*. My mind is lassoed onto hot cowboys. Yum. Ropes, spurs, yeehaw."

"Let the sex stuff go, will you? I don't need to have sex."

"Oh, but you do! Great sex is exactly what you need."

"If my libido were a car on the freeway I'd putter along in the slow lane."

"Because you've never had *great* sex." Tasha chuckled. "And for eighteen months, you've been in a deep freeze. Ticktock, time to climb down from your ivory tower, Rapunzel, and reclaim your sexuality."

"I dunno . . ." Kelsey fiddled with the hem on the wedding gown that had cost as much as a new compact car. Could Filomena get a refund?

"C'mon, you gotta have hot fantasies." Tasha's voice took on a sultry quality. "What are they? A little BDM? Role playing? Booty call in scandalous places? A park bench, a pool, a carnival carousel?"

"A carousel?"

"Hey, it happens."

"Tasha, did you have sex on a carousel?"

Her friend smirked. "Maybe. Once. I'll never tell."

Lowering her eyelashes, Kelsey tossed the rose bouquet into the trash on top of Clive's crumpled letter.

You were safe.

"Quit playing coy and cough 'em up," Tasha said. "Name your fantasies. Scottish Highlander in a short kilt and no undies? Or football player wearing those skin-tight pants? Fireman? Doctor? Construction worker?"

"The YMCA players . . ."

Tasha heehawed. "No more gay guys for you!"

"Hmm, there is *one* fantasy . . ." Kelsey mumbled.

"Just one?" Waving her hand, Tasha said, "Never mind, not judging. One is enough. What is it?"

Not what, *who*. "Forget it."

"Is he a real person?" Leaning in, Tasha's breath quickened. "A celebrity? Or . . ." Her voice dropped even lower. "Someone you've met in real life?"

Unbidden, Noah MacGregor's face popped into Kelsey's head.

In her mind's eye, Noah looked as he had the last time she'd seen him. Seventeen years old, the same age she'd been, and six-foot-five. Broad shoulders, narrow waist, lean hips. His muscular chest bare, hard abs taut. Her lipstick imprinted on his skin. Unsnapped, unzipped jeans.

Wild hair.

Wilder heart.

Rattled and rocked, her safe little world had tilted. Noah was so big, so tall, and he had a wicked glint in his eyes. An honest man, independent and sexy. One hot look from him had sent her heart scrambling.

That final night, they'd been making out on the dock at Camp Hope, a grief camp for children on Lake Twilight. That year they were both junior counselors, after having attended every summer since they were eleven as campers.

On the dock a blanket and candles and flowers. Courtesy of her romantic boyfriend.

Fever-pitch kisses.

They were ready to have sex—*finally*—when he'd jumped up, breathing hard. His angular mouth, which had tasted of peppermint and something darkly mysterious, was pressed into a wary line. Noah's thick chocolate-colored locks curling around his ears and his deep brown eyes enigmatic.

In her bikini, she'd blinked up at him, her mind a haze of teenage lust and longing. "What's wrong?"

"Did you hear something?" Noah peered into the shadows.

Propped up on her elbows, Kelsey cocked her head. Heard the croak of bullfrogs and the splash of fish breaking the surface of the water as they jumped up to catch bugs in the moonlight. "No."

Doubled fists, pricked ears, Noah remained standing, ready for a fight if one came his way. Prepared to protect her.

Her pulse sprinted.

Proud and brave and strong, he looked as if he were a hero from the cover of the romance novels that she enjoyed reading.

She'd fallen deeper in love with him at that moment. Head right over heels. Over banana splits at Rinky-Tink's ice cream parlor the week before, they had shyly said the words to each other. *I love you.* Then again when he'd carved their names in the Sweetheart Tree in Sweetheart Park near the Twilight town square. Several nights that summer they'd sneaked off for trysts after their charges were asleep.

They'd kissed and hugged and petted but hadn't yet gone past third base. Tonight was the night. She was on the pill. He brought a box of condoms. They were ready and eager. Kelsey reached for him, grabbed hold of his wrist, and tugged him to his knees. Their first time. Both eager virgins who'd dreamed of this for weeks.

Souls wide open. Hearts overflowing. Bodies eager and ready.

"Come . . ." she coaxed. "Don't worry, it's after midnight. Everyone is snug in their cabins."

Allowing her to draw him back beside her, Noah branded her with his mouth and covered her trembling body with his own.

Hot hands.

Electric touch.

Three-dimensional!

The night was sticky. Raw with heat and hunger.

Calloused fingertips stroked velvet skin. The boards of the dock creaked and swayed beneath their movements as he untied her bikini top.

Footsteps.

Solid. Quick. Determined. Immediately, Kelsey recognized those footsteps.

Filomena!

From nowhere, her mother was on the dock beside them, grabbing a fistful of Kelsey's hair in her hand, and yanking her to her feet. Kelsey's bikini top flew into the lake.

Angry shouts.

Ugly accusations.

Threats.

Curses.

Regular life stuff with her mother when things didn't go Filomena's way.

Mom, dragging her to the car parked on the road. She must have driven up with the headlights off. How had her mother known they would be there? Blindsided by the realization that Filomena must have been keeping tabs by tracking her every move via her cell phone, Kelsey's fears ratcheted up into her throat.

A hard shove and Filomena stuffed Kelsey into the car's backseat and shook an angry fist at Noah who'd followed them. Warned him to stay away. Promised litigation and other dire consequences if he dared to contact Kelsey ever again.

"Noah!" Kelsey had cried as her mother hit the

childproof door locks to prevent him from opening the door and springing her free.

Pounding on the car window, Noah demanded her mother get out and have a rational conversation with him.

Stone-faced, Filomena started the car.

"I'll come for you," Noah yelled to Kelsey. "I'll find you, and we will be together. We won't let her win."

Kelsey clung to that flimsy promise. Took it to mean something. Fervent hopes. Girlish dreams.

"Over my dead body," Filomena yelled.

"Please Noah, just go," Kelsey had said, half-afraid her mother would run over him. "We were just a summer fling."

All the fight had drained out of him then, and he'd stood in the darkness, fists clenched, face gone pale, shaking from head to toe.

Sobbing and shivering, Kelsey sat nearly naked in the backseat of her mother's Cadillac as Filomena sped all the way back to Dallas.

And Kelsey never saw Noah again.

Years later, out of curiosity, Kelsey searched for Noah and found him on social media, learning that he was a successful point guard in the NBA and married to a drop-dead gorgeous model—something she'd have already known if she had any interest in basketball. She did not friend him. It was far too late to rekindle childhood flames.

Lost hopes.

Empty dreams.

Ancient history.

Soon afterward, she'd met Clive, and that was that. But now, here she was, dumped and half-drunk, with nothing to look forward to but her mother's predictable holiday harangue. Plenty of reasons to hate the holidays. This year, she had little choice but to review her life's mistakes.

Ho, ho, ho. Merry *freaking* Christmas.

About the Author

LORI WILDE is the *New York Times*, *USA Today*, and *Publishers Weekly* bestselling author of eighty-seven works of romantic fiction. She's a three-time Romance Writers of America RITA® Award finalist and a four-time Romantic Times Readers' Choice Award nominee. She has won numerous other awards as well. Her books have been translated into twenty-six languages, with more than four million copies of her books sold worldwide. Her breakout novel, *The First Love Cookie Club*, has been optioned for a TV movie.

Lori is a registered nurse with a BSN from Texas Christian University. She holds a certificate in forensics and is also a certified yoga instructor.

A fifth-generation Texan, Lori lives with her husband, Bill, in the Cutting Horse Capital of the World, where they run Epiphany Orchards, a writing/creativity retreat for the care and enrichment of the artistic soul.

Discover great authors, exclusive offers, and more at hc.com.